Revamped and Reloaded

Written by Joshua L. Edwards

Table of Contents

FORWARD – SOME NOTES FROM THE AUTHOR 4

PROLOGUE – THE STORY BEGINS. 7

CHAPTER 1 – HARDLY A HINT 11

CHAPTER 2 – BREAKING BARRIERS 36

CHAPTER 3 – CONFESSIONS OF THE HEART 59

CHAPTER 4 – CONFESSIONS OF A CRUSH 81

CHAPTER 5 – TRUTHS AND CONSEQUENCES 110

CHAPTER 6 – IT'LL BE ALRIGHT 134

EPILOGUE – WRAP UP 141

Forward – Some Notes From the Author

I began writing this story years ago, shortly after breaking up with a girl named Michelle. She had shoulder length blonde hair, glasses, and huge tits. Like a Double D cup. She also had a tendency to lie and a low I.Q., which I found out later. She had come over to talk to an acquaintance of mine while I was eating breakfast, and I noticed that she had an ace bandage around her forearm for her wrist pain. I helped her rewrap her arm and sorta fell into her blue eyes. Now, she ended up giving some guy a hand job only 3 days into a relationship, lied to me saying she was at her Aunt's all night… why I needed to even know where she was, is still a mystery to me, and in the end it was her friend Megan who told me the truth. She broke up with me over Gaia Online and I started the story.

Frankly at that point I was bored with my classes and with my life. So I started writing. It began as just a short chapter involving a young lad and his sister experiencing sex with each other for their first times. I posted it on adultfanfiction.net and after a bunch of reviews came up asking me to keep writing, I wrote a second chapter, and a third and a fourth. I was actually about ½ way through the work when I told my roommate of the story's success. He, being the jealous manipulative fuck he was, told me that it was disgusting and I shouldn't write such filth. This was coming from a guy who would sit in the living room looking at gay cub porn and jack off but swear to god he wasn't a pedo or gay because cub porn didn't count.

Anywho, I turned around let my readers know that there was some disapproval, and after asking for more feedback regarding the situation, I was given 135 messages and thumbs up to keep the story going and say "Fuck you." To my roommate. Needless to say, he wasn't pleased.

Then shit really hit the fan because AFF.net wanted me to put their disclaimers on my work. Basically they wanted themselves to be taken out of any liability. I was like "Um no. If you are hosting my work, you have to take some liability. I'm more than happy to tone certain aspects down, but if you're hosting the work, you have to take some liability." And when I put in my own disclaimer, they told me "Put in our disclaimer or remove your work." So I removed it and took it to Hentai Foundry.

Hentai foundry was a great site for the time I used it, and then they put out a notice, pulling down anything that was remotely having underage characters in there. Didn't matter if they were involved or not, or had a young person just standing there doing nothing, it got pulled. So my work got pulled. I launched around the web looking for new sites that would host for me. But obviously getting it on a regular site that won't mess with me constantly is too much of a chore, so now this version is available for you to buy. Thank you for the purchase, by the way.

So where does this story start? It starts with a brother and sister, in a classic scene. Yes this story contains incest, beastiality, forced sex, and violence. It takes some time ago, in the Mid 1990's, During summer break. Originally the main characters were all underaged, but with the internet being policed like it is, I'm editing that. The story, though changing the basics of Age, are now pretty much the same as they have always been.

Before I begin in on the first chapter, a couple points have to be made.

This story is a work of complete fiction and though some of the characters may physically resemble people in real life, the people as written are made up. The situations are made up. Any similarities to reality are completely by coincidence.

Prologue – The Story Begins

My name is Joshua Timothy Swartz. My friends call me Joshua, or Josh. My family calls me Josh, or Joshy if they tend to want something. I'm 6 feet tall. I weigh 158 pounds. I have very short red hair and green eyes. I like to stay shaved but I'll let my beard and mustache grow out from time to time. I'm fairly muscular but not overly muscular and I spend my mornings jogging for about 2 miles a day. I spend my afternoons either gardening, or at my part time job helping people fix their electronics. I only do it part time because I don't really need the money. I'm 19 years old and have a twin sister. Her name is Heather Lily Swartz. She's as tall as I am. She's never had a boyfriend to my memory, but she's definitely into guys. Her favorite actor is Patrick Stewart and I've heard her say on occasion if he was 40 years younger then she'd date him, even with the bald head. I have two other sisters one younger and one older, who look so much alike despite their ages could also be twins my younger sister is Rebecca Sarah Swartz and My older sister is Rachel Sally Swartz. Rachel is 24, and Becky just turned 18 by the time this all started. We all live in a big house with our Mother, and thanks to a lot of money that my father left behind when he died to each of us, we don't have to want anything. Now I said *MY* father and not our *father* for a reason. Becky and Rachel have a different father from Heather and I but my Mom, Natalie, has always been kind of secretive about our fathers. Why? Well I didn't actually know at the point that I'll be starting in on the story. I find out all of that soon enough. At the point this all started though, I knew that Rachel and Becky had a different dad, making them my half-sisters.

Heather, my twin sister, was a bit of a tomboy during high school, and again, didn't have a real boyfriend but I had seen her figure plenty of times, and she did have a nice one. You know, flat stomach, nice sized tits… and I'm a bit reluctant to admit this, but I know that she's always shaved clean. I know this because when you live in a house with 4 women it comes up in conversations or you walk in on it at least once. As for her figure, she wasn't overly curvy, and had more of a tom boy build in muscles. I have seen her plenty of times accidently walking in on her, or seeing her in a bikini to know that. Plus, Heather never really kept anything from me. Now growing up, I wasn't the type of guy to get a girl easily. Or rather I didn't try. It wasn't that I wasn't interested, it's that well, my father died when I was still in middle school, so I didn't have someone I could really get some know how from and as for me just trying, there was always just one girl that I wanted to date. Well more than one, but the others… well one died due to a murderer finding out that she was a witness, and the other was my twin sister, but I had always heard it was wrong to date family so I never said anything to her. Now the remaining girl was a girl who lived down the street. She had dark skin, brown eyes, long black hair and drove me absolutely nuts to be around. I knew I wanted to date her from a young age. Well, I figured it out like any boy, I got a glimpse of her developing body at the time, and got turned on. It was only after that when I analyzed every time we had been together and realized that I was in love with her. But every time a guy asked her out, which I never did, she'd reply with a "You're not good enough, trust me." And then there was rumor going around that since her mom was a drill instructor that a guy would have to impress her first.

So during my high school years I never really had a girlfriend and during my first year of college it was pretty much the same thing. I mean I got flirted with a lot, and having Heather around always trying to hook me up with her girlfriends was nice and all but just wasn't me. I always ended up just turning them down when they finally asked. I didn't want to be tied down, but at the same time I did. Okay so I feel like I've been jumping around a bit, and I have, really. So let me get back on track here. Heather, growing up with, was a bit hard on me at times. Well how can it be like that? You've always heard twins are close? Well, it's true Heather and I really didn't keep secrets from each other, but Heather, and only Heather at first, noticed my uncomfortableness around the house when she would wear something revealing or skimpy and tease me with it. My two younger sisters would pick up on this in their teenage years and share in Heather's fun of teasing me.

Okay, now I think I might of peaked your interest about that, and I'll get into that soon. Let's move one to Rachel and Rebecca. Both of them, though having stunning bodies just like Heather, never wanted boyfriends. Why? Well I'm not to sure, but they always told me that they didn't have time for the drama. Rebecca or Becky as I called her once sat down with me and told me that if she got a boyfriend then she'd have to work him into her life somehow. Then there's the fact that he'd probably cheat on her because she wouldn't let him get any because she was waiting for marriage, and then they'd break up, and she'd be upset and it was just too much. I know my best friend, Johnny, asked each of them out originally, but they all turned him down. Poor guy.

Okay, so I've covered my sisters, and my crush, let's move on. My mother. Her name is Natalie and she's 40 years old. She had Heather and I when she was 22, but she won't talk about my father or my half-sisters' father. Why? No one knows. Alright. We get our red hair and green eyes from her, except, Becky and Rachel have dyed their hair to other colors. So my mom is a woman you'd consider a milf. She may be 40, but she has a tight toned body, with no visible stretch marks, and C-Cup tits. I've done her laundry tons of times, and as a teenager you notice that shit. Any who, yeah attractive mom. She works as a lawyer. Yeah Mom is a lawyer, Dad is dead and left me a shit load of money…

Okay, now that the introductions are out of the way, let's get to the story.

Chapter 1 – Hardly a Hint

I yawned as I opened my laptop. I was definitely ready to go to sleep and a good session with my hand was all I needed before hand. I could pull out my flesh lite and enjoy some time with it, but you ever use something so much that it losing its intrinsic value? Yeah it was like that for my flesh lite. Yeah I love the feel of the tight school girl pussy that it was supposed to mimic but at the moment it wasn't enough. As for my laptop, it was an older laptop but at the time it was top of the line but it definitely worked for what I used it for which was mainly to look at porn. My laptop was only 8 inch or something to that effect, but I kept in wonderful condition. It was silver in color except the keyboard which was blue. I had gotten a custom keyboard some time ago for it, after breaking some keys. Don't ask, long story.

My bedroom was a large room easily 12x15 or 14x18, somewhere around there. The walls were blue and covered with posters from my favorite TV shows, which were mainly anime. Thankfully I had found a person on the internet that could do mail order from japan. This was back in the day before the internet was more than dialup. Heck even my laptop which you would consider a fossil was top of the line back then.

I was lying across my bed, which stood next to my bedroom door. I never locked my bedroom door at night when I did this, for some odd reason. You would think I would in a house of four women, but no. As I brought up my favorite porn movie of a skinny Japanese girl who would get covered in cum then get creampied, my twin sister, Heather, came in the room shutting the door behind her. She made her way over to my cabinet and began shuffling through my VHSs.

She had her long red hair down, and was wearing only a t-shirt. And I do mean only a t-shirt. When she bent over, I glanced over to see her naked ass and pussy. She was hairless as usual. I kept my eyes on that beautiful pussy of hers which when looking at it, I could tell that she was aroused. Her outer pussy lips were puffed out, and the inner lips were glistening from her own juices. I could almost…

"Joshy? Where's that porn?" Heather asked. I was snapped back to reality.

"Which one?" I asked.

"The one in costumes? You know the Japanese one where they're supposed to be super heroes or something and end up getting tied up and… Oh wait here it is!" Heather said, bending over a little more. Her shirt rode up to just under her tits as she bent over. And my boner throbbed for attention and I was half tempted to whip it out and show her what she had done. She stood up and turned around. She blushed a bit. "Sorry, didn't mean to flash you." She said. I wasn't sure if she was lying or not. She walked over to me and bent over letting me see right down her low cut v-neck top. I could see her beautiful breasts and it was killing me not to reach out and start groping her right there. She loved doing this. She loved just turning me on, thinking I wouldn't be able to react in any way sexual. "Did you enjoy seeing it?" She asked in a seductive tone. "Your twin sister's pussy?" She asked. "With it dripping her juices? With her just wanting to be penetrated by a guy for the first time?" She set the tape on the far side of the bed and climbed on top of my bed, seductively biting her lower lip. She reached out and closed her laptop. "Well?"

"Actually, yeah. It turned me on a lot." I said blushing. I can't believe I said it. I just admitted to my twin sister that she turned me on. "It's not like I haven't seen you before." I said. "You walk in here nearly every night, usually in skimpy clothing, to raid my porn." I said trying to brush it off. "Wait. First time? I thought you were giving it up to Johnny tonight." I said. Johnny had been her boyfriend for close to a year, and she had been planning on giving him her virginity tonight for over a month.

She sat back in a normal manner and got an angry look on her face. "Ugh! That bastard! I went over to his house, ready to surprise him at his window and guess what I saw." She said.

"What?" I asked kind of shocked that Johnny would blow it with my sister. Johnny had wanted to be her boyfriend for as long as I could remember, even when I had tried dating his younger sister just so that we could go on double dates. When Heather finally broke down and told him yes, I thought he was going to hit the roof.

"I'm so angry about it, that I can hardly speak. I'm sorry, Joshy, I'll talk about it later." She said. She reached out and grabbed the tape and slipped off my bed. "Thanks for letting me borrow this, you've got the best stuff." She leaned in and gave me a soft peck on the cheek. I wasn't sure what to make of this. Did I just ruin a chance at getting laid? Wait, why was I even considering getting laid? This was my twin sister!

'Damn! I'm a sick fuck for even considering this!' I thought to myself, but then I cut myself off. She was attractive, and practically naked. I reached out and took her by the wrist before she could walk away. "Wait, Heather." I said, letting my cock do some of the thinking. "I think you need to talk about this before you go off and do what you have to." I said.

"Oh, Joshy, that's so sweet." Heather said. She set down the tape on my bed and climbed on, snuggling up to me. "You always know what I need." Oh I knew what she needed and I needed it too, but I wasn't sure if I'd let myself cross that line.

"So tell me what happened." I said, wanting her to at least get it off her chest.

"Okay, so there I was, wearing that Halter Top mom hates, and a pair of shorts, and I was outside his window." She said. I knew which top she meant. It was the one that showed off her upper stomach and her made her tits look bigger. "So I peeked inside to make sure he was in there before I knocked and I saw him naked on his bed, but he wasn't alone. Jessi was on top of him, riding his cock. I didn't want to believe they were having sex at first, but I could clearly make out his cock as she rode him."

"Really?" I said, kind of surprised. Jessi had always been the shy one and even when I dated her in high school, I couldn't even get her to hold my hand, so it was kind of surprising that she'd give it up to her older brother.

"Yeah. She was bouncing on his cock for a while, and I was glued to it. I felt myself get so wet that I almost had an orgasm in their back yard." Heather said spreading her legs a bit. She lowered her hand to her pussy and began teasing herself without even looking down. "Then she pulled out and he got up, and she got into a position on her hands and knees and he started doing her from behind. He fucked her for a while before pulling out and putting it in her ass."

"Wow, he really put it in her ass? No prep, no lube? I doubt it was her first time then." I said.

"I noticed that too." Heather said. "I watched as her tits swayed from the motions. And found myself getting hotter and hotter. I wasn't sure if I should interrupt or not, and call them out on the situation." I was getting hotter and hotter myself, and noticed my hand was now up my sister's shirt, massaging one of her tits. "When I watched his cum dripping out of her, that's when I left and came back home. I walked the entire way, trying to come to terms with him cuming inside his own sister." She said as she placed her hand down my shorts and grabbed my rock hard dick. I was surprised at this, but not as much as when she turned her head and gave me a passionate kiss. Afterwards she pulled back and blushed brightly, removing her hands as I did mine. "I'm so sorry. I… I… never…" She stuttered. In my mind I wasn't sure what to do, and was probably as confused as she was, but my sex drive took hold and I grabbed a hold of her, and pulled her into a passionate kiss. When we broke the kiss this time, she was the first to speak. "Wow. I never thought… I mean this is insane, but it feels right." Heather said.

"I know." I said, confirming that it wasn't one sided.

"I should go. We can discuss this later, when we're both thinking with something other than our bodies." Heather said as she pulled away reluctantly.

"I don't want you to." I said.

"And I don't want to go. I want you to make love to me, dear brother, but that's my body talking, and not my mind. I have to be sure of myself if I'm gonna take that step with you." Heather said.

"I understand." I said.

"I know you do." Heather said. She grabbed the tape and got off my bed. She turned back to me when she reached my door. "I'll talk to you later, okay?" She said. "Hope I didn't torture you too much."

"Nothing that a session with Rosy Palmer and her five sisters can't handle." I said as I put out my hand.

"You perv." She said before turning back to the door and opening it. Becky was right there and pushed past her as Heather left. Becky closed the door and sashayed over to my video cabinet, after the same thing Heather was. Her hair was loosely tied in a ponytail and was dyed black.

"Hi Joshy, just came to grab some porn." She said openly like it was nothing. She was wearing a pink see thru nightie, which hid nothing. While yes, the top part around her chest was a darker material, it was still see thru, and like Heather she wasn't wearing any underwear.

"You all need to get your own collection." I said. Becky, hearing this, turned back around. She quickly grabbed the straps of her nightie and pulled them down pulling down what little covering she had for her chest, letting me see her beautiful breasts. They were an A-Cup, something she was proud of. In her view, how many girls can say they still have small tits at her age? Honestly, I was in awe. As many times as I had walked in on her, or had done her laundry, this was the first time she had let me see them on purpose. Again, my cock was aching for attention.

"But then we couldn't come in here and tease you." Becky said as she slowly walked over to me. Becky was a bit deeper with the teasing before today, bringing things close to too far, then pulling back at the last second, so I mentally prepared myself as she climbed on my bed. "And if you weren't my brother, I could pay you back in ways other than teasing." She whispered.

"Oh you would huh?" I said. "I don't believe you, Becky. I think you'd be having fun teasing me even more."

"Oh you do?" Becky whispered. "And what if you had enough teasing?" Becky loved hearing me talk dirty to her, telling her what I would do, I've told her a million different ways that I would've fucked her at this point, and it was always more than enough to get her to back off usually.

"Well the first thing I'd do is force you up against the door." I said. I watched her hand trail down between her legs as she got closer to me. "Then I'd lift up your nightie." She let out a soft moan. "Then I'd start by licking your nipples, teasing them and sucking them until they were nice and hard." I whispered.

"Oh yeah. Tell me more, big brother." She said as she started to pant. I couldn't believe it. This time was different from the others, she was actually masturbating to what I said.

"Then after your nipples were nice and hard, I'd slowly lick down to your pussy." I said. She let out a whimper. "I'd start by teasing you, licking and sucking your pussy lips before attacking your clit with my tongue." She bit her lower lip. "When I was sure you were wet enough I'd move back up to your mouth and kiss you, sucking your neck would begin as I massaged your tits and then only when I was sure you were close, I'd start teasing your pussy with the tip of my cock." I said. Suddenly she reached into my shorts and grabbed my hardened member. She pulled it out and looked at it. Her eyes went wide.

"I don't know if you'd fit, Big brother. You're pretty big and I'm still a virgin." She whispered as she looked into my eyes. She had never done that before either. She was being either extremely brave or she really wanted me.

"Oh, We'd get it to fit, your natural lubrication would help and if you were fully aroused you could probably get me in. But like I said, we'd start with some teasing with the tip." I said, shifting my tone at the end to a more seductive one. This was going further than I ever expected and there she was, just slowly jerking me off. "Then after you begged me, I'd slowly push inside you, taking your virginity." I said.

She let go of my dick and laid on the bed with her body in the opposite direction of mine. She hiked up her nightie around her waist, keeping her top pulled down, then slowly spread her pussy lips, letting me see her virginity was indeed intact. Her pussy had a light brushing of red hair and she was fully aroused. Her outer lips were swollen with anticipation and she was wet between her legs. She slipped a finger inside her tight hole and moaned softly with one hand, while rubbing her clit with the other. I sat there in awe with my throbbing dick out. "Keep going, you're doing great, I just really need to get off." She said.

"Did you want me to actually do this stuff to you?" I asked.

"No... I... just... let me get off like this then I'll be good." She said. Needless to say, I was a bit disappointed. My cock was throbbing and wanted her attention. I knew what I should do if I wanted to take it further.

"Okay, so I'd start out slow, seeing how deep I could get in you, and how hard I could thrust." I told her. She bit her lower lip again. "Then I'd spin you around and start taking you from behind, not caring that people could hear us pounding you from behind against the door. I'd make sure that once I was taking you from behind, I would be doing it hard and fast." I said as I lowered my head without her noticing. I moved in close to her pussy and as she switched to teasing her clit, I put my mouth on her lower lips and began licking.

"HOLY SHIT!" She yelped as she felt me lick her pussy. She grabbed the back of my head as I kept licking. "Oh my god, Joshy, I never thought it'd be like this. It feels so right having you be the first guy to ever touch me like this." She moaned as she continued letting me lick her wet pussy. I moved from the lips to the clit, and began teasing it with my tongue. I couldn't believe it. I was eating my little sister's pussy. My little sister's pussy was the first one ever I was eating. "Joshy, I'm almost there. Come here." She said. She grabbed the back of my head, forcing me to stop licking and pulled it to her mouth to passionately kiss her. As she did, my body was pressed against hers, and I could feel her juices squirting all over my cock and balls. The feeling was intense, and I was having a hard time not shoving my erect cock inside her pussy as hard as I could. She broke the kiss and felt me against her, because her next move was to carefully move me off of her and onto my back. "That... was... hot. But you're not about to get laid, Joshy." She said, but before I could say a word, her mouth was around my cock. Even though this was a first for me, I enjoyed it thoroughly. The way she teased my head and licked my shaft, and with all the stimulation I had, I didn't even get a chance to warn her before my cum was erupting into her mouth. She swallowed every last drop down then licked my cock clean.

"So if this happened. Where would you cum?" She asked.

"Well with one final thrust, I'd cum inside your pussy, not caring if my incestuous seed made you pregnant or not. Cause I'd know you'd want it again and again after getting it once." I said in a seductive tone.

"Mmm, I thought you might say that." As she jerked my cock a few times to get it hard. "You know that was another first for me. I've never given a guy head before." She said. "And my orgasm, it's never been that intense." She said, breathing heavily on my bed. "Joshy, I don't know how you learned to talk like that, or eat pussy like that, but if the rest of your love making is anything close to that, the girls out there are really missing out."

"So, do you want to finish up? And have sex?" I asked. Wow, I had some balls. Forget the fact that this was my virgin sister who had never done anything like this before, but I was ready to actually fuck her and cum inside her.

"Got a condum? Cause I'm not using protection." Becky said.

"No." I said.

"Then not today, Joshy." Becky told me.

"Still want to find a porn to get off to?" I asked.

"No, but I think I owe you a favor." Becky said. "And I mean besides seeing me naked." She sat up and leaned towards my ear. "Cause anytime you wanna see me naked, I'll let you. Just don't tell anyone."

"And anytime you wanna hear what I'd do, why don't you come and visit me?" I said, sitting up and pressing my hand against her pussy. She gasped before pulling it away.

"Another day, maybe we'll do more. I'm just not sure if I wanna go all the way and let you cum inside me." She told me. My hand was covered in her juices. She got up and walked over to my dresser and grabbed a wash cloth. She quickly cleaned herself up with it, then after adjusting her nightie she tossed it in my hamper and walked back over to the bed. "This'll be our little secret." She whispered in my ear before leaving my room.

'Holy shit.' I thought to myself. 'Did that really just happen?' I looked at my hand, still wet with her juices. Yeah it had happened. I began jerking off after sniffing her juices, with that hand. Oh how good it felt having her juices seeping into my cock.

After finally relieving myself, I realized I had jerked off to the thoughts of screwing both Heather's and Becky's brains out. At first I told myself it was wrong, but then it occurred to me, maybe they weren't teasing me because they thought they could get away with it. Maybe they were teasing me because they actually were attracted to me in a way that they, in a sociological sense, shouldn't be. I could ask Becky about this later, and I'd probably be given a straight answer. I cleaned myself up and changed my bed linens so that I could get some rest. I quickly checked my email and found one that had just come in from Becky. Becky had sent me an email? I opened it, not noticing a rar file attachment at first. It read:

Joshy,

Sorry I made you do that for me earlier. I'm not sure what came over me. If you don't want to do that again, I'll understand, but if you wanna do more and slowly work into this, I'm all for it. Take your time to decide what you want. I wouldn't want to stand in the way, but just to help you make a decision, I've put together a rar attachment for you. It should help in giving you some inspiration for next time.

Xoxo

Becks

I quickly turned my attention to the attachment and downloaded it. I forced my Virus scanner to skip it since I knew the source and unzipped it to a folder on my desktop. I opened the folder to find 13 pictures of Becky, slowly stripping out of the nighty then up-close shots of her breasts, nipples, virgin pussy and asshole. Holy shit. I could've used these half an hour ago, but closed the folder, set it to hidden, so it vanished and got ready to pass out. Becky definitely wanted more. Frankly, I was sort of surprised that I was the first one that she really showed interest in. But I wasn't about to look a gift horse in the mouth, and soon sleep took me.

The next morning my alarm clock went off and I was up quick and ready for my morning jog. I headed out the door and began running down our street towards the wooded path that lay just beyond it. The property was owned by Mr. Stricker and he had given me permission to use it to do my daily training. "As long as you don't repeat anything that you see in there or get hurt I'm fine with it." He had told me when I was 12 or 13. Of course I didn't know what he had meant until nearly a year later when I ran up to a manmade pond in the back. Well I say manmade pond, but it was more like a hidden in ground pool that he kept nice and clean. When I had first encountered it, I found him fucking my English Teacher Mrs. Kravis. When he found me gawking at the site of the naked 30 year old teacher, he explained that he was a swinger as was his wife and they'd often have parties or get together using the tool. Mrs. Kravis wasn't too keen on having one of her students see her in such a manner, but after that I certainly paid more attention in class. She wasn't the only one I caught with the Strickers either, and it made me see adulthood in a different light. As I ran up to the pond on this morning though, Mr. and Mrs. Stricker were skinny dipping together.

"Hey Folks!" I yelled as I jogged up. "How's the water today?"

"Oh hey there Joshua! It's nice, come on in." Mrs. Stricker said.

"Oh no. I know what you're gonna want me to do when I get in there." I said with a smirk. "I don't have time for that kind of stuff today."

"Really? You know as often as we've offered you it, you never seem to want to get laid, Joshua." Mr. Stricker said. "We've got some pretty young things coming over later who would just love you, I bet." He said as I sat down on a rock next to the pond.

"Actually, I wanted to ask your advice." I said.

"Our advice? Now what advice could you possibly want from some old perverts like us?" Mr. Stricker said. "Wait, is this about a girl?"

"Yeah, sort of." I said. It wasn't easy to ask, but if I could talk to anyone it was them. "What do you two think about incest?"

"Well you've got me by the balls now, Joshua. The woman swimming with me, who I fucked all night is my sister." Mr. Stricker said. I was kind of shocked by that. His sister? The woman I had known as his wife since I was a kid was his sister. "So what do you want to know?"

"Well let's start with the obvious, you two have had kids right?" I asked.

"Before you get into that. No, No deformities, and they're all smarter than we could ever pray to be." Mrs. Stricker said as she leaned over the side of the pool. "Why? One of your sisters been fucking you?"

"No, no. But…" I started.

"She's getting interested. I told you those four were like pees in a pod. Didn't I say that?" Mr. Stricker said.

"Yeah you said it. You also said the reason you thought you never saw him with a girl or them with a guy, was cause you thought they wanted to fuck each other but weren't sure how to get started." Mrs. Stricker said.

"No, That isn't true for me at least. Incest isn't something that's been on my mind at least not until last night. I've always had a thing for Caitlin." I said.

"Oh that youngin? Cute little black girl down the road." Mr. Stricker said. "I'd love to show her how much experience comes with age, if you get my drift."

"Yeah. But last night," I took a breath before explaining "Heather came in the room to get some porn to do some angry masturbation and we ended up groping each other and making out, then Becky came in my room looking for porn, and I was turned on, and then Becky started by flashing her tits at me, then we started talking dirty and…" I said.

"And what? Nothing wrong with two adults fooling around." Mrs. Stricker said.

"She masturbated in front of me, then I ate her out, then she gave me a bj, and then she sent me an email later stating that she wanted to do more, but she wants to take it slow." I said. "I just wanna know, is the confusion of all of this gonna go away?"

"Trust me, Joshua. She's in for a treat when you finally give it to her. She's recognized that, but she's a bit scared. That's why she wants to take it slow." Mrs. Stricker says. "It'll be less and less confusing as time goes on. You'll both get into it and things will just sort of explode from there."

"Really?" I asked.

"Trust me." She said. "That's how it was for Bert and I. When I finally gave it up to him it was like a part of me had been filled that no one else could give to me, and though I still have many other men fuck my brains out, even at my age, Bert is still the best at not only pleasing me but filling my heart. Just take your time, you have no reason to rush."

"Thanks." I said as I got up.

"You sure you don't want a bj. or a handy-j before you run off?" She asked.

"Nope, I gotta get back and start my gardening." I said.

"Okay, don't work too hard." She said. I turned and began jogging back. It was a mile back home, and the two of them helped me to clear my mind. Funny how advice can do that for you.

I made my way inside and found myself almost running into Rachel as I headed for my morning shower. She had just gotten out of her shower and only had a towel draped around her body. She was pretty much physically identical to Becky except for the freckle beneath her right eye. It almost looked like a tear sitting there. She, like Becky, had tan lines from tanning in our back yard. Hard to believe that she was older than Becky, but I never had really thought about it, instead my mind was saying 'Hey, you've seen her naked now.'

"Morning Joshy." Rachel said as she walked up to me. "I heard you and Becky had a good time last night." She whispered as she got close to my face. She gave me a kiss on the cheek. "Thanks for whatever you did, 'cause she went right to sleep when I got in to our room. Usually she spends hours masturbating to porn."

"You're welcome, I guess." I said.

"Listen, I might have you repeat the performance if I'm ever having trouble sleeping." She said.

"Did she tell you what happened?" I asked.

"No, she didn't, she wouldn't say. She just said you two spent time together and it was very erotic, then went to sleep." She said. Well this opened up some doors for me.

"And you're fine with this?" I asked. She put her left hand on my chest then traced down the center with her pointer finger.

"Considering how much masturbating she needs to do before she can usually fall asleep? I welcome any help that she can get." Rachel said.

"So what if we fucked?" I asked.

"So what if you did? I don't care if you and Becky are fucking. But you must have been pretty good to calm her down. And I'm serious about that. I may just need you to fuck me one day if that's what got her to calm down." Rachel said. I was flabberghasted. Rachel was openly admitting that she'd fuck me.

"Well we didn't fuck, but I'll keep what you said in mind." I said with a smirk. She smiled and walked around me and to her room. I made my way into the bathroom to get showered. The rest of the day was pretty uneventful until later that night. I did my gardening all day, and later that night, I laid down on my bed and passed out pretty fast. That night I dreamt about getting into a threesome with Becky and Rachel. I didn't even wake up when Heather came in to snag some more porno or when Becky came in and grabbed some too. The day had been pretty tiring.

But it had given me some new insight into my sisters. One of them didn't give a fuck if I had fucked the other and even would've been willing to repeat the process if she wanted to. The other, Becky, had trouble sleeping so she masturbated to wear herself out. This was going to help in ways more than I thought in the future.

Chapter 2 – Breaking Barriers

I awoke later that night for some odd reason and found myself walking into the living room in just my boxers. Heather was there under a blanket, with it pulled up to her neck just watching a movie. I had no idea what movie it was but I sat down on the couch next to her.

"Joshy will you snuggle with me, while I watch this?" She asked.

"Sure." I said sleepily. She lifted the blanket for me to get under and behind her without lifting it far enough to see what she was wearing. I snuggled up to her back and put my arm around her to realize that she was in a pair of spandex shorts and a bikini top. She let out a slight giggle as she got the blanket over us. Within a few minutes she wiggled her butt into my crotch as we laid there, I can only assume to try and get closer, but it was far from doing that, as my cock jumped to attention, sticking out of the front hole of my boxers. She felt it grow to its full size and let out a small gasp. She rocked her hips against me again, letting my cock slip into a wonderful position where it sat against her pussy and throbbed. Only the thin fabric of her shorts were separating us now and I could tell that she was definitely feeling it. My hand instinctively reached down to her crotch and my fingers began to rub her through her shorts. She pushed her crotch against my hand, as I rubbed her most sensitive spot through her shorts and kissed her neck. I began to actually smell her arousal as I moved my hand from her crotch, with a moan of protest from her, to her waist band. I didn't waste anytime slipping my hand in and starting to tease her naked clit. As I teased her she grinded against me, teasing my cock with her cloth covered pussy. With my free hand, I reached up under her bikini top and began massaging her breast. She let out a soft moan. Suddenly she stopped grinding on me, and arched her back, as I felt a hot liquid shoot against my finger as she squirted in her shorts.

"Oh god, Joshua." She moaned. "That felt beyond wonderful." She said as she sat up. She got to her feet, letting the blanket fall to the floor. I wasn't sure what she was doing at first, but then she stripped off what little clothing she had on, and I followed in suit. I repositioned myself on the couch and she laid down on top of me, before passionately kissing me. I couldn't quite believe how fast she was moving on this. The night before she hadn't wanted it, wanted to think with her mind and not her body. "Joshua, I can't stop wanting this. As much as I've tried to think of this, I can't come up with a good enough reason to stop. Joshua, I love you and I want this." She said as she reached behind me and positioned me at her entrance. "I want you to be my first."

She pushed her body back, taking the tip and only the tip inside her. It was just between the lips of her pussy, and I couldn't believe she was doing it. "Wait, Heather, what about protection?" I asked.

"I don't care about protection. I've always wanted you like this. I wanted to be your girlfriend even though society is against it, and I've always wanted to be the mother of your children." She said, blushing brightly. "I love you Joshy, in a way a sister shouldn't love her brother, and it feels normal." And with that, she sat up, impaling herself on my cock, burying it completely inside her virgin womb. Her naked body illuminated only by the tv, and I found myself in awe, and in love with my twin sister as she began bouncing on my cock, fucking me for the first time ever, both of our virginities lost to each other. She was right, it did feel normal. I put my hands on her hips and helped her bounce on my cock, when we heard a noise and stopped. We looked back towards the entry way of the room.

"Well I can't say I'm surprised. If anything I'm surprised you two took so long to do this." A voice said. It was our mom's voice and she became illuminated by the tv as she entered the room. She was only wearing a robe.

"You're... not mad?" Heather asked. My cock was throbbing inside her.

"Why would I be mad? We all have urges and your brother is a very attractive young man." Mom told her as she walked over to us.

"Because it's incest?" Heather asked.

"Honey, if it weren't for incest, none of you would be born." Mom told her. "Your father was my brother, and Rachel's and Becky's father was my cousin." I could feel Heather's pussy getting tighter.

"Heather, if you keep clamping down like that, I'm gonna cum fast." I warned her. Heather let out a soft moan and began bouncing on my cock again.

"I had always expected you to at least be fucking your twin sister, Joshua, and maybe your other sisters as well." Mom said.

"I haven't fucked Becky or Rachel yet, though they…" I started.

"Oh I know. Your sisters are very open with me." Mom said. "I know all about you eating out Becky and her giving you a blow job. I also know Rachel wants you too." My cock throbbed at this, and I felt myself getting close. "In fact Heather told me how she felt for you when she was ten and her descriptions of what she wanted to do with you were very… erotic."

"Really?" I asked Heather. All she did was nod as she closed her eyes, enjoying the feel of my cock.

"Joshy, I'm getting close." She whimpered. "I want you to cum when I do. I want to feel your cum spraying deep in my womb."

"You know you might get knocked up today. You're at mid cycle." Mom warned.

"I know. I want it." Heather said. "Joshy, I'm about to cum!" I grabbed hard on her hips and thrust into her with all my might. She screamed out as I did, and we came in unison. She was squirting in a stream out of her clit as she came. My cock was erupting like a fire hose with full pressure inside her. I could feel my cum spraying deep into her womb and filling it up. She collapsed on top of me, as I kept cumming, letting out a long moan as I did.

"Oh god, that felt so good." I said as my cock stopped spasming inside her.

"I never thought my first time would be like that." Heather said.

"I have a feeling that you're gonna have many more times like that with your brother." Mom said. I looked over to her and saw her robe was now open, and she was sitting in front of us practically naked.

"Mom his cock just felt so perfect." Heather said as she pulled me out of her. I just kept my eyes on my mother's body. Mom gave Heather a passionate kiss as Heather pulled herself off of me. What happened next really blew my mind. My mother climbed on top of me and began grinding her body against mine until I was hard again.

"I hope you've got enough left in you for another round." My mom said. "It's been a while since I've had a dick as big as yours inside me." She said with a grin. She and Heather kissed passionately again. "Hope you don't mind the rest of us sleeping with Joshua."

"Not at all Mom." Heather said. With that mom lifted up, positioned my cock and lowered herself on it. My mom's pussy was hot, wet and tight. Holy shit was she tight. Mom quickly began bouncing on my hard cock. She grabbed my hands and put them on her C-Cup tits. I couldn't believe it was happening. Like I said, my mom was a definite MILF. Any of my high school friends would've loved to have been in my situation right now. My mom rode my cock for a few minutes then pulled me out of her. I was kind of surprised that she did until she laid down and motioned for me to fuck her in missionary position. I was happy to do so, taking in the sight of her hairy pussy before doing so. As I fucked her, I sucked on her neck and massaged her tits. Soon I was grabbing her ass with both hands as I got close. I started to warn her but she just wrapped her legs around me and pulled me into a passionate kiss. I felt her juices squirt from her pussy, covering my balls, which pushed me over the edge and I came inside her as hard as I did with Heather. After I was out of breath and exhausted. My cock hurt from the sex, and I was dizzy.

"That felt so good, baby. Mommy needed that." Mom said seductively.

"But I might have…" I said.

"Yeah you might have just knocked me up, but I'm not too worried about it. Your sister is the same way." Mom said. "And the orgasm you gave mommy was just wonderful."

I slowly removed myself from my mom's cunt and the three of us got cleaned up and headed back to bed. I couldn't believe that we had just done all of that. I drifted back to sleep with the thought of my twin sister and my mother being knocked up with my child.

I spent the afternoon in the basement working out. I was on my back using my Bowflex to work my chest. I didn't even hear her come down the stairs, but soon found who I thought was Rachel at first, straddling my waist. She was wearing a pair of spandex shorts and a work out bikini top with her hair pulled back in a neat ponytail. I thought it was Rachel at first because Becky hated wearing her glasses but Rachel loved them, and this time, Becky was wearing them.

"So have you thought about the other night and the email I sent?" Becky asked.

"Oh, Becky. Sorry, thought you were Rachel." I said, letting the straps ease back.

"Wait... it was the blasted glasses wasn't it? Or has Rachel started teasing you again? I thought she stopped." Becky said.

"No, she still does it, just in a more... what's the word... sophisticated way." I said.

"How so?" Becky asked.

"Oh she'll do things like mounting my waist while I'm working out, in a skimpy bikini and then talk to me pretending that I'm not looking at her body. Or come to me with a question in very form fitting clothing and do a variety of poses that while not revealing would get a man's juices flowing. Why?" I said.

"No reason, I just might have to get some pointers from her. Any who, I might have mentioned something that night to her." She warned me.

"Yeah, she knows, so does mom and Heather. No one cares. You're an adult, Becks, you can do what you want." I told her.

"Yeah she came to me about trying some different methods of falling asleep and I can't think of anyone else to come to. So I figured the constant masturbation sessions I'm having are getting to me. I need to work out this extra energy." Becky said.

"Well why don't you?" I asked.

"Why don't I what?" She asked.

"Work out." I said.

"Would you show me how to use this thing then? That's why I came down here looking for you." Becky said.

"Sure." I said. I started showing Becky some of the basic exercises showing her which areas it would work out by touching her body. I didn't know if this was some roués for her to get me to grope her, or just she wanted to work out, but I was fine with both. I helped her stand up after showing her the basics. "So do you think that you'll be working out on the machine?" I asked as I wiped it down.

"Maybe. I'll see if I'm up for it." She said. "Why do you wipe it down?"

"Keeps it lasting longer and not smelling like ass." I said.

"Oh, that makes sense." She said.

"And regarding the other night, I'm perfectly fine if you need something along those lines again. I had done some soul searching and asked some people who know regarding these types of matters." I said. "So yeah, if you wanna pursue this kind of thing, just let me know." I said.

"People? What people?" She asked.

"Mr. And Mrs. Stricker." I said.

"Really, why would they have insight on that?" She asked. I leaned in so that I could whisper in her ear.

"They're brother and sister." I whispered. She grabbed my face and kissed me, passionately. I don't know how long she had been waiting to do that, but she did it. Her tongue soon found its way in my mouth and explored a bit before she broke the kiss, and looked up at me, blushing brightly under her cute glasses. It almost made me forget I was half a foot taller than her.

"I'm sorry, I should've asked first before doing something like that." She said.

"No, it's alright Becky." I said.

"It's just, I've had a crush on you since I was a kid, and that's why I always shied away from guys. They just didn't measure up to you." She said. "I'm not sure why I'm saying this now, but when I took your cock in my mouth the other night, I knew I wasn't gonna find a man to measure up. It just felt perfect having you in my mouth." She turned away from me and looked towards the floor. "Josh, I love you in a way a sister shouldn't love her brother." She said. What could I say? I felt like that for her. I wanted to be in a relationship with her... It felt odd for the moment. I loved her. I put my arms around her, and took the chance to reach up her bikini top to fondle her tit. I massaged it, before teasing the nipple a bit making her moan in pleasure.

"Becky. You don't know how much I want you. I wanna put you over my weight bench right now and fuck you until you scream." I whispered. "But what about taking it slow?" I asked as I pulled my hand away so that she could turn around and face me.

"I was wrong, big brother." She said turning back to me. She wrapped her arms around my neck and kissed me again, passionately, consumed by her desire. She jumped up, wrapping her legs around me. I put my arms around her and my hands on her ass as we made out. She broke the kiss. "You really want to stop?" She asked.

"No." I said reaching down to her shorts, which were made of spandex. I grabbed at the seam that went down the center, right where her pussy was.

"Wait what are you?" She asked as I pulled and tore a hole in them, large enough for my cock to have access to her pussy. I pulled down my shorts as she stayed wrapped around me, and quickly started teasing her outer lips with the head. "No! Don't tease me!" She whined.

"I want to hear you tell me what you want." I said.

"I want you to take me. I want you to fuck me as hard as you can and fill me up with your cum. I've wanted you to do it since I was a teen. I wanted you to fill me so full and knock me up so I can walk around with a big pregnant belly and let everyone know I was yours." She moaned. "Please, fuck me!" She begged. I arched my hips and slowly slipped the tip in between her pussy lips, making her moan. I grabbed her hips and forced her down the rest of the way on my cock, making her scream out. "Oh gods yes!" She yelled. I walked us over to the work out bench and laid her on it, and began pounding away at her pussy making her moan with every thrust. "Joshua! I'm gonna cum!" She yelled. I picked up my pace, as I felt her squirting, out of both holes. Her clit was spraying like a hose and her pussy was shooting her juices all over my balls, which only made me cum harder inside her. Again, I was cuming like a fire hose was spraying. "Oh my god Joshy. That was wonderful." She said with tears flowing from her eyes. I kissed away a tear and noticed a mark under her eye. I wiped away the make up covering up a large freckle. Remember, the only difference I've ever seen between Rachel and Becky is that one freckle.

"Rachel?" I asked.

"I'm sorry, I lied to you. I just wanted it so bad." Rachel said. "Becky and I came up with this whole idea for you to finally make love to me."

"I wish you hadn't lied to me, Rachel. I would've gladly fucked you senseless without the lies." I admitted. Somehow I wasn't angry or upset that I had been deceived. I was happy that she loved me this much.

"I love you so much, little brother." She said.

"I love you too, Rachel, but still you should've just been honest." I said.

"I know, but I didn't want to risk you saying no." Rachel said.

"I wouldn't have. I would've made it more memorable. I skipped out on a lot of foreplay because I thought you were Becky." I said.

"Well, you'll just have to pleasure me with foreplay next time." She said matter of factly. I pulled out of her, making her moan in disappointment but her legs were still around mine, and after a moment, she knew what I was up to when she heard a rip and I slipped the head of my cock into her tight asshole. "Wait, Joshy, have you ever done this before?" She asked.

"Nope." I said.

"Be gentle." She said.

"I will." I said as I slowly began slipping my cock into her ass until I was buried to the hilt. Her ass was as tight as her pussy. "So was this Becky's idea to disguise yourself or was it yours?"

"Mine. Becky just went along with it." Rachel admitted.

"So is she disguised as you, up in your guys' room?" I asked.

"Yeah." She gasped as I began slowly slipping in and out of her ass.

"You wanna help me with something then?" I asked.

"Only on one condition." Rachel said.

"What?" I asked.

"You gotta promise me that we'll keep making love like this in the future." She said.

"Anytime you want it." I said, pulling out of her ass and kissing passionately. She released her hold on me, and took my hand as she sat up. She was blushing brightly as she examined her shorts, realizing the holes didn't show normally. She stood up and led me up to her bedroom door. She stopped, ran back to the bathroom and came back, her cover up fixed. She opened the door to find Becky laying on Rachel's bed. I had pulled up my shorts before we opened the door. Becky was wearing a pair of Rachel's glasses and reading a thick book. She was dressed in a see thru white baby doll top with black panties and no bra, and a pair of socks that had the tops pulled down to cover her ankles. She had a bit of makeup on to simulate the freckle beneath her eye. Rachel led me over to the bed, and before Becky could protest, she had her panties off, and had my head in between her legs, licking at her clit.

"Rachy (Pronounced: Ray-chi)! I told Joshy what you told said before about wanting to have him make love to you, and he's all for it." Rachel said trying to sound like Becky. Again before Becky could protest in any way, Rachel had pulled her into a passionate kiss and began groping her body as I ate her out. It wasn't long before her pussy convulsed and she squirted into my mouth. I got up and put the tip of my dick inside her pussy lips.

"Joshy wait!" She tried to protest, but Rachel pulled her into another kiss. Becky kept one eye open and kept it on me as I slowly slid my cock entirely inside her. Her eye went wide as she felt my cock pressing against her cervix. Rachel broke the kiss with Becky who was panting hard not sure of what to say or do. I had taken her virginity like Rachel had wanted me to do, but she wasn't Rachel, she was Becky, who had wanted me to use a condom. "I… Josh…" She muttered.

"What's wrong, Becky? I thought you wanted this too." I said before leaning in and sharing a passionate kiss with her. I was keeping myself as still as possible. Mainly because I knew that if I started really having sex with her, I wouldn't stop for a condom.

"Nothing, I wanted this." She said, trying to act like Rachel for a moment, but then she realized I had called her by her real name. "Wait, you called me Becky." She said as I got back in a kneeling position. I slowly pulled my cock from her after reaching in my pocket and pulling out something. I opened the package and slipped the latex cover over my cock before I leaned back in.

"Yeah, you also wanted me to use a condom. I wanted to let you feel it first before putting it on." I said.

"How'd you know?" Becky asked. "That it was me?" she contined as I teased her slit momentarily then slid it back inside her. She moaned as I bottomed out again.

"Rachel's make up wiped off when she came hard during our session in the basement." I said.

"Wait? Session? I thought you were just gonna give him a bj?" Becky panted at Rachel.

"He didn't really give me a chance. He sort of took it to this level because he thought I was you." Rachel admitted before kissing Becky. I began thrusting in and out of Becky's tight pussy. Becky put her hands on my back and raked her nails across it as I pounded away. I began thrusting hard and fast as her pussy got hotter and hotter. It was overwhelming. Usually the condom would stop the heat until a woman was at her peak, or so I've learned since then, but Becky was truly aroused as I fucked her.

"Oh god, I'm close." Becky said.

"Me too." I said. I was holding back as much as I could until she grabbed me, pulled me into a passionate kiss and began grinding her hips against mine. I couldn't hold out any longer. She wrapped her legs around me as my cock went off like a firehose again. After a moment or two, she released her deathgrip on me, and I humped a few more times before pulling out. "Wow, that was terrific Becks." I said, her eyes growing wider. She was surprised, and tears were flowing down her cheeks.

"Oh my god." She said covering her mouth. Rachel turned to see what she was looking at.

"Well, I'd have to say it's been taken out of your hands, now Becks." Rachel said. I looked down to see what they saw. The condom was bunched up around my cock. It had burst while I was having sex and when I came, I had filled my youngest sister's womb with my incestuous seed. Becky's head fell back on the pillow as I sat down and pulled off the broken condom and threw it in the trash.

"You don't get it Rachy!" Becky cried, as she pulled herself into a sitting position with her knees to her chin.

"What you don't think you're ready to be a mom? It's not like you're alone in it! You have Joshy, Heather, Mom and Me to help. Your life isn't over!" Rachel pointed out. "Besides that, we're all ovulating today, and Joshy has cum in all of us! You heard Mom and Heather!"

I was stunned. All four of them were ovulating and I came inside them all. Any one of them could be pregnant now, and we wouldn't know for sure. Becky was still upset, but calmed down as soon as I put my arms around her. "I would love for you to be the mother of my children, Becky. I love you." I said. She pulled back and kissed me, not as a sister would kiss a brother but as a girl would kiss a boy she loved.

"I love you too." She said after breaking the kiss. Becky and Rachel began talking openly in front of me. I determined that incest definitely was running in our generation in our family. I wasn't sure how this whole pregnancy thing might play out, but I was definitely up for it. Becky just needed some more emotional support, and Rachel was happy enough to give it to her. The two of them had been fooling around for about a year in secret, and had always talked about getting in my pants apparently. Though it had been Rachel who really wanted to get pregnant right away and not Becky, though both were definitely a possibility now.

As the two chatted away about what would happen next, I got up and made my way downstairs to the bathroom to get cleaned up. I took a hot shower and got ready for a nightly jog. I got suited up in my running gear and threw my work out gear in the washer before heading to the door only to be stopped cold in my tracks. Heather was standing there, completely naked, in front of the door.

"I wanted to warn you." Heather said.

"Of what?" I asked.

"I don't want you going over to Johnny's looking for trouble. I ended the relationship with him. I didn't say what I saw, just told him that I've found someone else. So he might come to you and ask." Heather said.

"Okay, Heather." I said before giving her a kiss on her lips. Johnny lived right up the road from us, so there was definitely a possibility that I ran into him on my jog. She stepped aside and I started out the door and down the steps, before too long, I saw someone in front of me on my jog and recognized who it was. It was Jessi. I took her by the arm as I jogged and she realized it was me and I wanted her to come with me. We jogged to Mr. Stricker's wooded area. It was time to play my hand with Jessi.

Chapter 3 – Confessions of the Heart

I stood there, staring into Jessi's blue eyes. Her hair was short and black with a small section dyed crimson. She had black lipstick on and black eye shadow and eyeliner on. She had a black athletic T-shirt on with a pink bra, which I could tell what color due to the straps hanging out. She had D-Cup breasts, and wore a mini skirt which poofed out a bit and black sneakers. In short, Jessi was an emo girl, before it became cool to be one. Nowadays, "Emos" or "Goths" are everywhere, and Jessi wore both very well. Very cute, and very sexy, especially with her Cleavage. She was very attractive for being a year younger than me, and I would've hit that in an instant if I had been given the chance in high school.

"So you wanna tell me what happened? Or should I just start on what I know?" I asked.

"What do you mean?" Jessi asked her eyes not leaving mine.

"Okay, that's fine, I can tell you what I know. You've been fucking your brother." I said.

"J.T.! How dare you! I haven't fucked anyone!" Jessi scolded me.

"Heather saw you two in Johnny's room, the other night. The two of you were having sex." I said. Jessi covered her mouth and her eyes widened in disbelief.

"J.T., your sister was only half right when she told you that." Jessi said. Now she had my interest peaked. She sat down on a large rock and grabbed my hand. She pulled me towards her, then pulled on my arm, pulling me down, She hiked up her skirt and pulled aside her panties, letting me see her pussy. She spread her pussy lips showing me her proof. Her hymen was still fully intact. "J.T., I've never even had a finger inside me. I don't use tampons, I use pads. Nothing has ever been inside my pussy. Your sister saw my half-sister…. Er…. Cousin… actually I'm not sure what her relation counts as. She's the daughter of my father and my aunt." Jessi said before covering herself back up.

"Wait? Your dad is… was… in an incestuous relationship with his sister? And now your brother is too?" I said, kind of stunned.

"Yeah. I don't pretend to know what's going on, but it's kind of hot." Jessi said. "And as for my involvement. I… um…" She started to say. She sighed before closing her eyes tightly and blurting out: "I wouldn't fuck anyone but you J.T.! I love you!" She opened her eyes wide in shock again and covered her mouth with her hands again. She couldn't believe what she just said to me. "I'm so sorry, J.T., I didn't want to blurt it out like that, but I've been waiting to tell you for so long how I felt. I was crushed when we broke it off. I wanted to take things slow, but not telling you ended up pushing us apart. Again, I'm sorry, J.T., I wish things had been different. You might still…" She said before I interrupted her by placing my lips against hers, kissing her passionately. She definitely returned the kiss, and wrapped her arms around my neck. She put her hand on the back of my head, holding my lips against hers as she slipped her tongue into my mouth. She let her tongue explore my mouth and even wrestled hers with mine. The passion she released into the kiss felt like she was trying to get out her feelings since we had broken up, trying to show me how much she wanted me, or wanted to be with me, or how much she loved me. Slowly we broke the kiss and put our foreheads together. "Wow." She said. "I never thought our first kiss would be like that."

"Really? Maybe you should've let me kiss you sooner then." I said jokingly.

"Kiss me? J.T., I'm ready to let you fuck me. If we weren't in the woods right now, I'd be naked and trying to get you hard." Jessi said. I was awe struck. Jessi wanted me in more ways than one and she was still a virgin. "But if my parents found out…"

"Actually your parents wouldn't care." I said. She pulled back and her eyes grew wide.

"What?" She asked.

"When we were back in high school, I had a long chat with your dad about us dating before we hooked up and at the time, he insisted that I use a condom our first time since we were still in school." I told her.

"Wow, daddy said that?" Jessi said. "Well, let's just go talk to them then." She said. She got to her feet and I stood up. We walked, hand in hand out of the woods and back to her house. Her house was brown in color, and a ranch style with an added second floor. She led me inside to her dining room where her father, mother and another woman were doing bills at the table. "Daddy?" She said sweetly.

"Yes sweetheart." Her father said without looking up.

"You remember J.T. and the talk you had with him back when we dated last?" Jessi said, testing the waters.

"Yes honey?" her father said.

"Well what if I told you that he knocked me up?" She asked.

"I'd tell you that I was happy for my little girl and I know he would make a great father, why?" Her father said still not looking up.

"So you wouldn't be mad if we had sex?" Jessi asked.

"No, because I know you love him undeniably, sweetie and I know he feels strongly for you." He said, finally looking up. "Otherwise you wouldn't be here, asking me for permission to have sex with him. Honestly, I thought you two had already done it."

"Mom, what do you think? Are you okay with it?" Jessi asked.

"Of course sweetie. Your dad is right. The heart wants what it wants." Her mom said.

"And the body loves pleasure." The other woman said. Jessi giggled at that.

"Okay. Thanks Mom, thanks daddy." Jessi said before pulling me back out of the house. We began walking towards my house to clear things up with Heather, when we ran into Johnnie and their half-sister/cousin who were walking towards us and talking.

"Oh hey Josh." Johnny said. "Jess? Are you two dating again."

"Yep." Jess said even though we hadn't set anything in stone. "By the way, Josh, this is my half-sister, Sarah." Jessi was right. They could be twins. Sarah was dressed in a loose t-shirt and a pair of shorts with a pair of sneakers. Her lipstick was red, and she didn't have much else on for makeup. Of course all I could think about was how to get these two into my bed at the same time. She looked me up and down.

"Jessi, he's kind of cute. I think you picked a good one. I hope he's just able to please me, like my man." Sarah said.

"Yeah I heard about all of that. Never thought you were into incest, Johnny." I said.

"Neither did I, until Sarah took my virginity in front of our parents." Johnny said, his face turning red.

"I was trying to make a point that I'll do what I want, but then he was so good, I just couldn't stop." Sarah said, before placing a kiss on Johnny's cheek.

"You know, it would've been nice if you had let Heather know." I said.

"Who's Heather?" Sarah asked.

"His twin sister. She and I are sort of dating." Johnny explained.

"Were. She told me that she broke up with you." I said.

"Yeah, she did. Sorry about all of this. I don't know why she broke up." Johnny said.

"Oh she was going to let you take her virginity, and spotted the two of you fucking... you should close your curtains." I said.

"Oh shit." Johnny said. "I'm never gonna live that down with her."

"Well not enough to get her virginity, cause that's gone." I said.

"Wait, who?" He asked.

"Oh you know, some guy." I said, referencing something we used to say back in high school when referring to ourselves but being innocent to those around us.

"Holy shit man." Johnny said. "Does Jessi know who it was?"

"No, Heather will probably let her know in a few. We're going to my house now to clear her name." I said. "Cause these two ladies look too much alike."

"Well, she is my little sister, and I have to say, if she'd let me, I'd make love to her all night long." Sarah said. Jessi blushed brightly. Now I was really turned on. If I could get Jessi to agree to a threesome in the future, I might really enjoy myself.

Jessi grabbed my hand and pulled me past them towards my house, tired of waiting for us to stop chatting. She didn't say a word and I thought she was pissed off until we reached the porch. "Fuck," She said turning towards me. "Now I've heard it all. I knew she was fucking him, but her wanting to fuck me, and you fucking your sisters?" She said. Oh fuck, she knew. "Or is it just Heather? Be honest with me, J.T.." She said.

What could I say? I could've lied and said that I didn't. I could've told half of the truth, or I could've been honest. She was waiting for an answer and she deserved one. "And my mother too." I said quietly.

"That's kind of kinky." She said with a smile. "Who knew the guy I was hot for could be such a freak. I might have to get them into it with us." Holy. Shit. Dude. This was insane. She took me by the hand and took me into the house, not even taking a second glance at Rachel and Becky who were making out in the living room on the couch as we passed them. She pulled me straight to Heather's room and threw open the door. Heather was laying on her bed, in a red t-shirt and blue pair of panties, reading a book with her knees bent. She looked up from her book, marked her place and set it on the bed beside her, as she tried to control her rage. Her hand was shaking as she set it down and then she pulled herself into a seated position with her legs over the side of the bed. She stood up and walked over to Jessi.

'Here it comes.' I thought as I watched the two of them stare into each other's eyes.

"Heather, I know your angry…" Jessi said.

"Damn, fucking straight I'm angry, bitch." Heather said still trying to control her rage.

"Young lady! Language!" I heard my mother call out from her bedroom. Still amazed that she can hear from that far.

"Heather, I wasn't the one who fucked my brother. I'm still a virgin." Jessi said.

"Then who the fuck was it? Your twin sister?" Heather asked.

"Well, half-sister." Jessi said.

"And what proof do you have of this?" Heather said.

"Well you could check my pussy, like Joshua did, and see my hymen is intact, or see how tight I am, but that's not really proof. But I have better proof." Jessi said. She grabbed Heather by the hand and pulled her and me out of the room at a quickened pace. She brought us down the street to her house then pulled us around to Johnny's back window, where Sarah and Johnny could be easily seen, as they were just starting to get heavily into groping each other.

"Holy fucking hell." Heather said before turning to Jessi.

"Heather, you've been my friend for years, and your brother has always been my biggest crush. I'd never betray you both like that. I'd never do anything like that unless you both were somehow in on it. I care for you too much to do something that would hurt you like that." Jessi said.

"Jessi, I'm sorry I thought it was you. She looks just like you." Heather said.

"I know." Jessi said. "It's been kind of freaky but she's my half-sister, through my dad and his sister."

"Wait. Your dad had an incestuous baby with your aunt?" Heather said.

"Yeah, and it kind of turns me on." Jessi said.

"Oh!" Heather said before turning to me. She instantly noticed that I was still watching them as Sarah pulled off her shirt, revealing her D-Cup breasts. Johnny immediately went to sucking, licking and groping them. "Josh." She said. I didn't respond. "Josh!" She said again, but no response as I imagined myself enjoying them. "JOSH!" She almost screamed at me, this time punching me in my arm. I finally turned my attention to her. "If you want to enjoy tits, you have two pairs here with you. So let's go home and enjoy each other." She said with a smirk. She turned to Jessi. "I'm sorry for thinking that you'd do that."

"It's okay, she gets mistaken for me a lot." Jessi said. Heather took both of our hands and led us back to the house, and into her room. She locks the door behind her, and pushed Jessi onto the bed onto her back. Before Jessi can say a word, Heather's face is buried in her crotch, licking and sucking at her pussy through the fabric of her panties. Heather began to undress herself as she ate out Jessi. "Oh god, why are you licking me like that?" Jessi asked.

Heather pulled away. "You have to understand, my brother is the most important person to me, and as far as I'm concerned, he's my boyfriend. If you want him, I'm gonna have to approve." Heather said. I was shocked that she'd be so protective over me screwing Jessi. Heather pulled the fabric aside and began licking her naked pussy.

"Oh Heather!" Jessi moaned throwing her head back as my twin sister began sucking on her clit. Jessi began bucking her hips as she reached her peak of arousal, but before she could cum, my sister stopped and Jessi let out a groan of disappointment.

"Get undressed." Heather said, and Jessi blushed. Heather, by this point, herself was only wearing her panties. Jessi grabbed the bottom of her shirt as she sat up and slowly lifted it over her head, revealing her pink bra. She reached around to the back of it, and undid the clasps and let it fall forward a bit. She grabbed the straps and pulled it off her arms, and sat for a moment, with her naked breasts exposed. She was a 30D cup with small nipples and areolas the size of a half dollar. They were beautiful and perky. She reached down to her skirt, and slowly slid it off with her panties, showing off her completely naked body as she took all of her clothing and dropped it on the floor. All that remained were her socks, and shoes.

Heather helped her remove them, and I have to admit, my cock was so hard at this point that it hurt. I looked at her body, her flat stomach, her beautiful tits, and her naked pussy and I wanted her. Heather turned to look at me. "Well, Joshua, I have to say, I approve of you fucking her, but..."

"But?" Jessi asked. I kept looking at her. It was like I was a pent up teen in high school again, and I just wanted to fuck her brains out. My cock was throbbing at the mere sight of her naked body, and screaming at me to fuck her.

"I don't know if you're girlfriend material for my brother still. Things are on a different level now." Heather said.

"What do you mean? A different level? I mean, I'm willing to fuck him. Hell, I'm willing to let you both fuck me. I know about the family secrets and I'm up for just about anything." Jessi protested.

"Trust me, I understand that, Jessi. I realize that I got you all worked up, but there are more factors than the family secrets here." Heather said, taking a seat on the bed. "First off, you'd be fighting for his heart against all of his sisters. Because all of us want him to be exclusive to us, then there's Caitlin." Heather explained.

"Caitlin?" I asked as I started to get undressed.

"Oh yeah, Caitlin's had a thing for you since we were kids." Heather said. "And then there's the pregnancies that are bound to happen." Heather said. "I mean, even if you were just to be another 'friend with benefits' to him, could you honestly say you'd be willing to deal with the fact that one or more of us might be pregnant by Joshua? I mean, he only used protection with Becky, and that condom broke."

"Heather, I hate to sound like a heartless bitch..." Jessi started as I sat down on the bed. She got to her knees, and knee walked over to me, pushed me back and straddled my waist. She took my cock in her hand, raised herself up, positioned my cock at her entrance and slowly slid the head of my cock between her pussy lips. "But I don't think who J.T. dates is any of your business and..." She said before forcing herself all the way down on my cock. Her pussy was unbelievably tight as she forced me to bottom out in her. I could feel the walls of her vagina hugging my cock, trying to adjust to its size. I could see a small amount of blood trickle from her as if she had just cut her hand. Her pussy felt like I had just dipped my cock in molten lava and I swore if I stayed that way too much longer I was gonna spray my cum like a garden hose inside her. "I'm gonna do whatever it takes to make J.T. mine. Whatever it takes. I love him more than I love anything else." She said looking into my eyes with tears in hers. Heather smiled as Jessi began bouncing on my cock. I was stunned. Jessi pressed her lips to mine, and gave me a kiss more passionate than she had ever given me, then broke the kiss and told me she felt odd. I was about to warn her that I was cuming but she kissed me again as she began squirting, covering my lower body in her juices and as she did, I exploded inside her, my cum shooting out of my cock like it never had before. I could feel her womb expanding as I came, trying to adjust to take every drop of it inside her like it wanted to take every last drop. "J.T., I think you just came inside me." She said as I continued to cum.

"I still am…" I groaned as my balls continued to empty inside her.

"Jessi…" Heather started. "How long ago was your last period?" She asked.

"A couple weeks, why… oh. Well I did say I wanted him, and I wouldn't mind if I had his child." Jessi said with a giggle at the end. Again, I was stunned. She just sat there, with my cock fully inside her, her womb now as full as I could get it with my cum, saying she wanted a kid by me.

"How much did you cum inside her?" Heather asked me. I turned my head to look at her.

"I don't think I've ever cum that much, sis." I said.

"You realize she might have just gotten…" Heather said and then stopped herself. "You don't care if she got knocked up?"

"Oh I do. I care that any of you girls got knocked up by me, but she didn't care to stop, the only one who cared to protect herself was Becky and we all know how that ended up." I said as Jessi slowly raised herself off my cock, trying to not spill a drop of cum. She then repositioned herself and began to clean my cock with her tongue, which in turn felt great. She licked up and down my shaft, ignoring the head at first, but then engulfed my cock in her mouth, licking all of our juices off of it. Once she felt she was done, I was rock hard and my cock was covered in a nice layer of her spit. I didn't realize why until she straddled me again, and this time positioned my cock right at her asshole. Before I could say a word, she had shoved my cock all the way in her ass. She turned herself around so I could look at her back as she rode my cock and again, I could see blood trickling down my shaft. She rode me for a while as I felt even more of a build up in my cock. Her ass was as tight as her pussy was but she was constantly moaning. She rode up and down, and I could feel her asshole, which clenched my cock like it didn't want it to be pulled out, tight around my cock. She was playing with her clit as she rode me, enjoying the feeling.

"Oh, J.T.! I'm getting close!" She cried out. I could feel her ass clenching down harder as she rode me.

"Me... too..." I panted.

"Cum inside my ass! I want you to fill me with your cum! I love you!" She yelled out. I grabbed her hips and thrusted hard against her and then held her there as my cock spasmed. "YES! JOSH! YES! FILL ME UP WITH YOUR CUM! MAKE ME YOURS!" She screamed as she came. Heather, this time, was in shock. After I finished cumming I let go of her hips, only for Jessi to pull out and spin around to get me hard again. She dropped to her knees in front of me, placing her breasts on my waist. She put my cock in between them, squeezed them together, surrounding my cock. She began moving her tits up and down my shaft, getting it hard quickly, then she plunged it into her mouth with no concern that it had just been in her ass. She bobbed her head up and down as she sucked me off, jerking off my cock as she stopped to lick it all over.

"Oh god, Jessi, how did you ever learn this?" I asked.

"I've been dreaming of making love to you for a long time, J.T., and like I said, whatever it takes to make you mine. I want you to seriously consider my feelings for you." She said before going back to sucking my erect cock. She was really enjoying every second of getting me off. I couldn't believe it, it was just awesome. My cock began to throb again. My balls tightened, and she began to deep throat me.

"Jessi! I'm gonna!" I warned she plunged it in as far as she could. My cock exploded again, and my cum was pumped right down her throat. She swallowed down as much as she could, but soon it filled her mouth and began to overflow, out of her mouth. After swallowing down what was left, she licked her face and my cock clean again.

"J.T.…. Josh, I want you to know, whatever you decide, whatever! I am yours, and yours alone for the rest of my life. My pussy, my ass, my mouth, only you will cum inside me. Only you will be inside me. I could never love another person as much as I love you." Jessi said. She got up, walked over to Heather and kissed her passionately. "Thank you for getting me ready for him. You can really eat a pussy well." She said after breaking the kiss leaving Heather stunned. She picked up her clothing and pulled it on.

"Where are you going?" Heather asked.

"I'm gonna give Joshua some time to think over his position. I mean it's a lot to consider and figure out, bringing another person into this. He has to consider it from all angles." Jessi said as she pulled on her shoes and socks. She was fully dressed again. She fixed her hair and then walked out of the room.

I slowly stood up and staggered out of Heather's room. Jessi was right, I had a lot to think about. She had just given me sexual relief in ways that I never thought possible. I had filled her holes with my cum and still I wanted her more. I wanted her in my bed with me, I wanted her to stay with me, and I wanted her to make love to me. I wanted to make love to her. Wow, she had me hooked. I thought about what she said, about me making a choice. Then I thought about getting her and her half-sister in a threesome. Then I thought about both of them walking around with their stomachs big and fully pregnant by me. My cock was sore and my balls ached so much that I really didn't want to masturbate.

I soon passed out with all sorts thoughts running through my head. I ended up dreaming of Caitlin. Odd, because she had only been mentioned briefly. The dream was of me confessing the situation to her, and her telling me I was gross as her body shifted of her as an adult to her as a child, but 9 months pregnant, then she ran off somewhere, and I tried to find her, while everyone told me her baby was mine. Dreams are weird.

Chapter 4 – Confessions of a Crush

I yawned before rolling over and looking at my alarm clock. It clicked over showing exactly two minutes before it would go off and I would have to get up. I reached over and turned it off before pulling my legs over the bed. I sat there for a moment and scratched my head, then I stretched and yawned. It was gonna be a long day, and I had a lot to do, or at least a lot planned. I stood up and yawned again and walked over to my closet. I opened it up and looked in the mirror. For a 28 year old I wasn't bad looking. Besides the Five O'clock shadow, I had a relatively muscular build, 6 pack abs, nice pecks, all in all not bad, if it weren't for my short red hair being in bed head mode.

So let's see here, where was I? Oh yes, Jessi had just basically called my sister out on me deciding who I would date. All of my sisters and my mom had me cum inside them, and Jessi had me come in her pussy, ass and mouth. Becky hadn't wanted me to cum inside her, but the condom broke and after some time with Rachel she got over it. Jessi had decided that she also wanted to be a mother to my children and I was now standing there getting ready for another day. I knew I wasn't gonna figure this out over night, but damn was this a predicament. Then the thought had occurred to me, Heather had mentioned Caitlin was interested in me. Caitlin was my crush throughout high school. I quickly fixed my hair, grab a shirt and a pair of shorts, threw on my shoes, and made my way out of the front door, to start my morning jog.

"HEY JOSH! WAIT UP!" A voice called out. I turned around to see a young black woman running up behind me. She had a nicely sculpted body. B-Cup tits, flat stomach, nice hips and ass, and long black hair that reached down to her back. It was her! Her name was Caitlin Attah, and to be frank, I would've given my left arm, left leg, and left nut to date her in High School. She was smarter than most people I knew, but beautiful too, but to be frank, her mother was scary. Her mother was a boot camp instructor, and the general rumor that had went around is that you'd have to impress her mother. Though I was confident myself, I wasn't sure enough to try and impress her mom. I slowed down to let her catch up. She was wearing a grey work out bikini top with the Nike logo on it in the center. She was also wearing a pair of loose fitting shorts, which were black in color. She finally caught up to me, and we began jogging together.

"I didn't know you jogged every morning! This is so cool! I thought I was gonna have to do this alone!" Caitlin said as we began jogging together. I figured this was probably a lie, because Caitlin was friends with Heather and I knew Heather and her talked at length regarding me. When I questioned Heather about why they talked about me, she brushed me off with a 'No reason.' But I had heard Heather giving my morning schedule a few times to her, and honestly, if this is how it turned out, I really didn't mind. At this point, I knew I owed Heather a favor, because she knew how I felt about Caitlin. But then I wondered if Heather had called Caitlin and warned her to make her move because of Jessi.

"Yeah, I started it back in junior high school, when I was that scrawny guy, and figured it wouldn't hurt to go for a jog before my day started." I said proudly.

"It shows." Caitlin said, looking back at my ass in a more than obvious manner. I blushed at this as she looked at my face and smiled. "I was actually hoping on running into you this morning."

"Hoping or planning?" I asked as I slowed down to a walk. She slowed down with me and sighed.

"Okay, I guess I'm busted. I had planned it. I figured you probably overheard Heather talking and put two and two together, so I'm gonna try to be frank with you Joshua.." Caitlin said. She was breathing kind of heavy for a short jog, and it hit me that she wasn't used to the pace she had been keeping with me.

"Wait does that mean you're going to turn into a guy?" I asked with a smirk only to get punched in the arm. She didn't hit that hard but it sort of felt like when you get a shot, and you don't relax your arm.

"Bastard. Just stop so we can talk for a minute." Caitlin said. We both stopped and I turned to face her.

"What is it?" I asked.

"I want you to go on a date with me." She said.

My jaw literally hit the ground, like I mean those old cartoons where the bad guy would see a hot chick and his jaw would hit the ground, and his tongue would roll out like a carpet. I fell over. I didn't want to, but I fell over. I had blacked out the moment what she was asking hit me, and later opened my eyes to see her over me with her hands on my shoulders.

"Josh. Josh! Come on, wake up! I don't want the first guy I ask out to die on me!" She said as my hearing came back. I blinked.

"So it wasn't a dream?" I asked.

"Oh my god, don't scare me like that." She said as I sat up partially. She gave me a huge hug, throwing her arms around my neck and almost choking me.

She pulled back and blushed brightly, realizing she had just hugged me. Funny thing was I never pegged her for the shy type. I thought she was always really popular with the guys... wait... She had said...

"I thought I wouldn't ever have a chance... I mean the rumors in high school..." I started. "But here we are, and you asked me out?"

"Yes, silly. I just asked you out. Well, sort of... I told you I wanted you to go on a date with me, but that's semantics." Caitlin said as she pulled back. "And what do you mean 'rumors'?"

"Yeah, there was this rumor that you didn't get any dates because your mom was military and the guys would have to impress her." I said.

"You silly fuck, that's because I used to blow off guys left and right telling them they wouldn't be good enough… frankly I was waiting for you to try, but you never did." Caitlin said.

"What?!" I said. I was flabbergasted. My high school crush, the girl I had fantasized about not only having raunchy sex in every opportunity I could come up with as a teenaged boy, but also fantasized about marrying and starting a family with, wanted me to be her boyfriend all this time. "Why… why didn't you tell me?" I asked still stunned.

"I'm shy. It took me until last week to even ask Heather for your schedule. I don't know how I managed to get myself out the door this morning. And then when I saw you, I sort of threw caution to the wind and wanted to at least catch up to you." Caitlin said. She blushed even brighter which I didn't think was possible, she looked down as she let go of me. "So um…" She started but then started to mumble and fidget with her hands. She was genuinely embarrassed about asking me out. It was cute. Though I wasn't sure how to answer her. Would I seem like a creep if I just pulled her into a kiss to answer her? I mean she only told me that she wanted a date with me, not that she wanted a relationship. "Besides, when Heather called me up last night and told me… Heather warned me about what happened yesterday and what's been going on with you and your family. I know everything. I know you've been having sex with your sisters, and I know how much Jessi made you cum last night." She admitted.

She was in on it as was Heather! She didn't seem upset or anything, but she kept looking down. "Okay, so a date then? Where should we go?" I asked. She looked up at me and her eyes lit up like a kid at Christmas.

"Really? Even after you did all of that with everyone, you'd still give me a chance? How about we go get some coffee? I mean we're already out and about." She said with a smile.

"Sure." I said with a smile. She squealed with delight and hugged me tightly again, this time jumping in my lap with a leg on either side of me. She pulled back and kissed me. Then I felt her parting her lips and let her slide her tongue in my mouth. We sat there for a moment, making out, as we explored every inch of each other's mouths with our tongues. We finally broke the kiss a few minutes later and Caitlin slowly opened her eyes.

"Wow." She said with a smile. She was blushing again. "I've never done anything even close to this with a guy."

"You've never made out with a guy?" I asked as she stood up and offered me her hand.

"I've never even KISSED a guy before today." She said as I took her hand and she helped me to my feet.

"Wait, what? You can't be meaning you've never done anything what so ever with a guy? I mean your older sister Kira, and your younger sister Tamika…" I said. Needless to say I was a bit in shock. Her family, minus her mother had always had the reputation of being a bit promiscuous, but thinking back I hadn't seen her at Junior or Senior Prom. I hadn't seen her ever even holding hands with a guy.

"Have reputations that they're whores?" Caitlin asked as we started walking back to my house.

"Well, they did in High School." I pointed out. I had entered high school during Kira's last year and was in my last year when Tamika was just starting ninth grade. Both had ended up with a reputation of being a whore. Which I had only thought true because I heard Kira was caught in the girls bathroom giving a teacher head.

"That was back then. I mean, as far as I know, they're both virgins, but I've seen Kira give a guy head, and Tamika, well, I don't think it was fair that they gave her that reputation." Caitlin explained.

"Why not?" I asked.

"Well Tamika is shyer than I am when it comes to guys, or girls." Caitlin said but then covered her mouth like she just revealed a huge secret. "Don't tell her what I just said, please!"

"What? Why would I? How would that ever come up anyways?" I asked.

"Well, if she sees that I'm with you… she might… get jealous." Caitlin said looking down. We both stopped again. I turned to look at her. "She's had a thing for you too, for a long time, and one day we were talking and she kind of confessed that she had a thing for your twin sister as well."

"Heather?" I asked.

"Yeah, Joshua, I wanna be clear about something." Caitlin said turning towards me. She looked up at me with determination in her eyes. "I'm in love with you. I don't care if you're dating some other chick right now, I will win you over one way or another, and I won't stop until I do. And if it comes down to it, I'd be glad to prove my love in ways my sister could never come up with." She confessed.

"Caitlin." I said sternly before pulling her into a hug by her shoulders. "Let's just take things slow for now." I said softly. I felt her melt into the hug. "I'm not seeing anyone else, I'm single. And the only one I've even agreed to a date with is you." I whispered. I could feel her breathing heavily against me, like she had been holding her breath to hear those words from me.

"Joshua, you don't know how long I've been waiting to hear that." Caitlin said as she pulled back. I could see tears welling up in her eyes.

I wiped a tear away. "Why are you crying?" I asked. She hugged me tightly again.

"You silly fuck. You silly silly fuck." She said.

She took a few more minutes hugging me before finally pulling back with a smile on her face. How much had I missed that smile? In high school I had seen it on a daily basis. She had lived around the corner from me all my life and we had always been friends. I never thought she had wanted anything more than that and yet here I was, still holding this beautiful, intelligent, attractive, sexual goddess that I never would have guessed would give me the time of day for a date. My perception of her had been successfully shattered into tiny pieces. To top it all off, her 18 year old sister wanted me as well as my twin sister. The thought of the two of them wanting to fight over me was a bit… farfetched but it was true. I hadn't seen her sisters since high school and only had seen Caitlin in passing. But there she stood, just looking into my eyes and smiling.

To be honest, I wanted to take her into the woods and fuck her every way possible, then go find her sister to do the same. But I pushed it and the thought of anyone else out of my mind. I wanted her right now, and only her. The two of us eventually broke our embrace and made our way to my house, where I quickly ran inside to grab my wallet. I returned to have her just smile at me again, before we headed down the road hand in hand to the coffee shop. When we stepped inside she turned to me.

"I can't believe this is actually happening. You and I are on a date." She said.

"Caitlin? Why didn't you ask sooner?" I asked.

"Like I said, I'm shy." She said again.

"But you seem perfectly open to me now, I mean you confessed your love out there on the sidewalk." Joshua said.

"Yeah, but I didn't know you even felt remotely like I did." Caitlin said as she reached into her pocket and pulled out a hairband and quickly pulled her hair into a pony tail.

"You wouldn't believe how long I had a crush on you." I told her as we got in line.

"Wait, you? On me?" She said in disbelief.

"Yeah but with the rumors, I never figured that I could get you to agree to even coffee since I'd have to impress your mom." I told her. The line was moving slow and the coffee shop wreaked of old man cigars. You know, the cheap kind. Some old men were sitting at a table and one looked up towards us. He smiled.

"See Johnson? Those kids are getting along. They're even a nice couple, and they're interracial." The old man said. His companion turned his head and looked over to us, as we approached the counter and made our order. The old man got up and walked up to me, tapping me on the shoulder. I turned around to look at him. His hair was white on the sides, and dark on top. He had a white mustache and glasses. He wore a business suit.

"You kids look wonderful together. In my day, a mixed couple wouldn't be caught on the streets together without all sorts of people calling them heathens." The old man said.

"Why thank you." Caitlin said as she took a hold of my hand. "We're just glad we live in a day where we can have our fun without worrying about the injustices of the past."

"Well I'm Mr. Johnson. I run a special type of parlor that makes videos for the internet. If you two are interested in making some money, I could use both of you." Mr. Johnson said as he pulled out a business card and handed it to me. I briefly looked at the card which displayed his name and a company logo, and then pocketed it. We turned back towards the clerk who handed us our drinks then went over to a pair of recliner chairs and when I sat down, I was surprised to have Caitlin sit right across my lap.

"Comphy?" I asked, noticing now that her ass was sitting right on my crotch. I tried to ignore it, but my body would be fighting me on that point relatively soon enough if she didn't move. This was coming right out of one my teenaged masturbation fantasies very quickly.

"Happily so." She said before planting a kiss on my cheek. "I've always wanted to sit in your lap and with this clothing, I'm betting that you won't be comfortable long." She whispered. She was doing it on purpose! My eyes nearly bugged out of my head.

"You want me to get hard?" I whispered.

"Do you know how many times I masturbated to just the thought of this kind of situation and how it would play out, Joshua?" Caitlin whispered. Again I was flabbergasted. She just admitted to masturbating to not only to me, but to of situations that were similar to my own. I didn't know what to say to her. So I did the logical thing. I pulled her into another passionate kiss. I knew this would have an effect on my body, but didn't care.

"You wouldn't guess how alike we are, Caitlin." I whispered. Now I was all in. I wanted her to know exactly how I felt. She pulled her head back, her eyes went wide.

"You too? Wow. We really should've hooked up sooner." She said before taking a sip of her coffee.

"Caitlin, I had a huge crush on you all through our teen years. I think I first started falling for you when we were both at the lake together when you were twelve." I said.

"You mean back when I wore that blue one piece?" Caitlin laughed. "That thing was too big on me and kept falling off!" She stopped, realizing that I had seen her tits more than once that day, and started laughing harder. "That had to be a 12 year old boy's biggest dream."

"In more ways than one. That's just when I started to notice that you were, for lack of better phrasing, growing up." I admitted. "It was that experience that made me get to know you a bit better."

"I remember you followed me around every chance you got for a while, until we got to high school, then we drifted apart." Caitlin said.

"Well I'm looking forward to getting back into getting to know you again." I said before taking a sip of coffee.

"Well not much has changed. I got the job at Walmart, bought a car, and as of this morning found a hot guy to jog in the morning with." She said, the last part she added a giggle after.

"You think I'm hot?" I said in disbelief, almost choking on my coffee. I set it down on the floor next to us.

"Why wouldn't I?" She said. "I mean…" She says then starts blushing again. I was intrigued. Why did she find me attractive or 'hot' as she put it? She leaned up against me so she could whisper in my ear again. "I've seen you working out a couple times when I was over visiting Heather, so I've seen you without a shirt. I know you're pretty strong and muscular as well, you're actually the type of guy I find attractive in that sense. Plus I know you're pretty big downstairs, thanks to Heather letting me in on all the details about you." She said tracing a finger down my chest. "I hate to sound like a horney teenager here, but I've been waiting to see it for myself." She said, then she gave off a yelp, as my body responded. My cock was, at this point, throbbing, but not just from her words, but her touch, and her scent. Oh god, did she smell good. "I'm guessing I'm gonna get that chance pretty soon." She whispered with a smirk as I ran my hand up her inner thigh and into her shorts. I didn't touch her pussy though, I just kept rubbing up and down her thy as she kissed me.

"I think it's awesome we finally hooked up like this, but aren't we moving a bit fast?" I asked her. She shook her head like a little girl. My mind at this point was telling me to slow down. That I didn't want our relationship to be all about sex… not that we were anything official yet… but my body wanted to just pull off her shorts and start fucking her on the spot. It was kind of maddening.

"No, everyone's got a leg up on me so far in this thing." She said. Heather to the rescue again. I felt her manipulating this whole thing to change who I'd end up with. The question was, who was she going to manipulate next and who did she want me to be with? "Joshua, I don't want the date to end. I mean I know it has to, but, I want us to be more than just friends or fuck buddies. I could have any fuck buddy I wanted, but you… I've loved you for a long time." She said as she leaned in. Whoa, talk about moving fast! "I've loved you since you were that little boy who would throw water balloons at me. Now I want to be more than just the neighbor girl who never could express her feelings." She confessed. Then I realized it. For Caitlin, it wasn't about moving fast or slow, she had loved me a long time and now she had the courage to tell me.

I kissed her. What other reaction could I have? It was passionate, loving, and I held her as I did so. "Caitlin. I love you too.

I have for as long as I can remember. I want us to be more too." I told her.

"So, officially? What? Boyfriend and Girlfriend? Fiancés? Fuck buddies or Friends?" She asked.

"I'm still a bit indecisive about that still, is that alright?" I asked.

"I know you need time to weigh all the factors, Joshua. I just hope that I'm part of the choice." She told me. She definitely was part of the choice now, especially with my hand running up and down her smooth thigh. She took one last sip from her coffee and set it down on the table next to us and stood up, pulling away from me. She took me by my hand and pulled me up into a standing position and then pulled me out the door. She pulled me around the back of the building to an area that was wooded so we wouldn't be seen by anyone just passing by. She knelt down in front of me, and pulled down my shorts a bit, letting my cock spring free.

"Wow, bigger than I imagined." She said before taking it into her hand. I could feel it throb at her touch and she giggled. "You'll have to excuse me, I've never done this before." She said. "But I doubt that you're gonna wanna walk home with a fishing pole in your pants." She told me before taking it into her mouth. I was in heaven. Here I was, expecting my day to be routine, now instead with a woman I had loved since I was a kid who had finally worked up the courage to tell me how she felt, and on top of it, she was giving me head like an expert. She was licking the tip, swirling her tongue and generally making my cock feel great like she had been doing it all her life. I was loving it, and before long I felt an all too familiar feeling. I tried to warn her, but she wasn't letting up. Then I felt it, the release, cumming in her mouth, and watched her swallow it down like it was natural. When I was done, she pulled my manhood from her mouth and pulled up my shorts. She stood up and licked her lips. She hugged me. "I've wanted to do that to you for so long." She said.

During the time that she had been giving me the blow job the sky had turned overcast and now it was starting to sprinkle. "Well if we stay here were gonna end up soaked." I said.

"Why, Joshua, are you suggesting that we take this sexual interlude to your bedroom?" Caitlin giggled. Holy shit, she really wasn't fooling around when she said that she wanted to do this.

"No I'm just suggesting we get out of the rain." I said, not sure of what she was driving for.

"Deal, let's head to your house." She said. We began walking back towards my house, but took it into a harder jog as the rain came pouring down. Needless to say, by the time we reached my front porch, we were soaked. "Oh man! Where did this storm come from? It's gonna suck to head to my house in this."

"You're not going anywhere in this." I said turning back towards the street, which was now flooded. Caitlin turned and looked. Her eyes went wide.

"Holy shit." Caitlin said.

"Yeah, let's get into some dry clothes." I said as I turned back to the door and opened it. We stepped inside. Heather was sitting in the living room on the couch.

"Holy shit, you two are soaked!" Heather said before suddenly realizing that Caitlin and I were standing there together. "Wait! Caitlin? You actually caught up with him?"

"About time that I finally got up the courage to ask your brother out?" Caitlin asked trying to complete my twin sister's thoughts. Heather was wearing a tube top, which showed off her b cup cleavage. She had her long red hair pulled into a pony tail.

"Something like that." Heather said with a smile.

"And what happened?" Heather asked. The two of us were still dripping wet.

"Heather this can wait." I said, grabbing Caitlin by the hand and leading her into my room. I went into my dresser and found a long shirt for Caitlin and a pair of boxers. I grabbed a blue long sleeved shirt and a replacement pair of boxers for myself. I tossed Caitlin's replacement clothing on the bed, and stood there a moment aghast again. She had already stripped down taking off her clothing.

"How about a towel first?" She asked.

"Uh, sure." I said after pulling my jaw off the floor at just the site of her naked body. Her tits were firm, and her pubic hair was a thin strip. I grabbed a towel from the top of my dresser and tossed it to her, which she used to dry herself off some. Then she giggled at the fact that I was just standing there watching her dry herself off.

"Well are you just gonna stand there all wet?" She asked as she slowly walked over to me. "Or did my crush want me to dry him off?" She said in a more seductive tone as she got close to me. I'll be honest, I wanted to throw her on the bed right then, and start fucking her brains out. I wanted to do her in every position, fucking every hole she had until she was not only screaming from the pleasure but covered in my cum.

"Hey, how often does a guy get to see the girl, who he's had a crush on since he was a kid, completely naked? I was enjoying the show." I said before pulling off my shirt. She stepped back and watched me as I stripped. After I had pulled off my soaked clothing she tossed me the towel. I began toweling off.

"Oh yeah, now I see what you were enjoying. It's very arousing seeing you like this." She said with a smirk. I blushed, causing her to giggle. She sat on the bed. "Now I wanna set some ground rules for our relationship, cause I don't wanna feel like I'm a complete slut, but I wanna be with you boo." She said. My guess was she was starting to feel remorse for the BJ and being nude, but then why wasn't she getting dressed? "That thing in the woods, that was me takin' responsibility for my bad, you know?"

"Oh so you're saying you gave me that wonderful blowjob not because you love me, and want me, but because you gave me a hard on?" I asked, raising an eyebrow.

"Dammit Josh, stop poking holes in this. I want this to be real." She said. I sat down next to her, still naked. We shared a passionate kiss. "Okay. You have a point, but I don't wanna hear…" She started to say, only to press her lips to mine again. After breaking the kiss she smiled. "Okay, fuck it." She said. "I'm not gonna win this thing with rules." She said. "Just tell me you won't go off and catch something from some cheap whore."

"You know who I've been screwing… Why would I go off and find a whore?" I asked.

"Good point." She said. We kissed again, and she pulled us back into a laying position with me on top of her. I set the towel aside as we made out. I started kissing down her neck to her tits, and began licking and sucking at her nipples. "No, don't do that…" She moaned but held my head in place. I was getting hard fast, and wanted to return the favor for the earlier blowjob, so I kissed down her stomach to her pelvic region. "Wait, what are you?" She started to protest while I spread her pussy lips and found her clit. I began licking and sucking on it furiously. "Oh god!" She yelped. She moaned loudly after a moment or two as she squirted, spraying my face. When she calmed down, and stopped squirting, I grabbed the towel and cleaned off my face. I moved back up to her mouth and we kissed passionately. I took my cock in my hand and began teasing her outer lips. I slowly slipped the head inside her waiting pussy. "WAIT." She said.

"What's the matter?" I asked.

"It's not that I don't want it. Believe me I do. I want you to fuck my brains out." Caitlin said. "But I'm not on birth control, so do you have a condom?"

"Yeah, but…" I started. "When Becky and I used one, it broke, so I'm not so confident about what I have." I said.

"As much as I want our first time to be raw, I don't wanna get knocked up so fast." She said. "We've been waiting for years. I think we can wait a bit longer." She sighed. "Besides. I'm exhausted. I'm not used to getting up so early. So I tell ya what." She started. "I'm gonna get a nap, right here in my wonderful boyfriend's bed. You can lay with me if you want, but if the rain hasn't let up when I wake up, I'll rethink the condom thing." She said with a smile. Wow. My luck. I'm serious. First I get the girl I had been crushing on to go on a date, then blow me, I get her naked, in my room, in my bed and now she wants to take a nap, and if the rain doesn't let up, I have a chance having her for the first time bareback. If it does, I could always go for a quick drive to grab some kind of contraception.

"Okay with me, beautiful." I said before pulling the tip out of her. My cock ached to be thrusted inside her. It burned with a need to fuck her brains out. But my brain told me this was the best option for both our needs. I mean, I didn't want to be just knocking everyone up either, but that thought wasn't an unpleasant one. I sat up and handed her the long shirt and boxers and grabbed my shirt and boxers. She only pulled on the long shirt and tossed the boxers aside. I grabbed our wet clothing and walked them out to the dryer. I pulled the stuff out of our pockets and noticed the soaked business card. I put our stuff in and I turned it on and walked back into my room to find Heather and Caitlin talking.

"It was amazing Heather. I've never gotten off that fast" Caitlin said before looking up at me. "Hi hun." Heather looked back at me and licked her lips. I knew what she was thinking. She wanted a threesome.

"Hey, telling my sis about our dirty deeds?" I asked.

"Just going over the basics of you eating me out." Caitlin giggled. "I didn't tell her about the blowjob in the woods." Heather's head snapped back to Caitlin.

"Wait, you did what to him in the woods? I wanna hear about this. Did you get him off? Did you swallow? Did you like his taste?" Heather asked.

"Wow. Sis. Just wow." I said.

"Joshua, I'm just trying to make sure you have all the information. I know that you have a decision you're going to make, I just want you to make the right one." Heather said, turning her head back to me. "So, I hope you don't mind me asking." I walked over to the bed. I mean she was my twin sister, it was kind of embarrassing listening to my new girlfriend and my sister gossip about my sexual exploits right in front of me. I laid down on the bed, next to Caitlin, resting my head on a pillow. She looked over at me for permission.

"Tell her whatever you want. I mean, I can't get mad for you gossiping to your best friend about what we did." I sighed.

"Your brother is actually really big, especially when he's fully hard. I'll be honest, I don't know if he can get it all in me. I only had a couple inches of him in my mouth, so yeah there was still a lot sticking out, and I was surprised when he came in my mouth. He warned me, but I swallowed it down. He came a lot too." Caitlin said.

"Wow. Just wow. Sounds like you really enjoyed giving him head." Heather said. She leaned in and whispered some things in Caitlin's ear. Caitlin's eyes went wide and then she shoved my twin sister lightly. Caitlin and Heather looked back at me and shared a giggle.

"Well, regardless of what we may or may not want. I need a nap. Could you give me and Josh some time to sleep?" Caitlin asked.

Heather sighed and rolled her eyes. "Really?" Heather asked. "I mean you two have gone so far already and now you're just gonna take a nap? That's a jip." Heather giggles.

"Well you can't expect us to just fuck like Rabbits." Caitlin said with another shove but Heather got up and left the room as Caitlin pulled the covers over us, snuggled up to me and we slowly drifted into slumber.

Chapter 5 – Truths and Consequences

I woke up a couple hours later to the abrupt buzz of the dryer finishing, finding myself on my side with my right arm underneath Caitlin. Normally that wouldn't be a problem, but my left arm was around her, and up her shirt which was hiked up, and my left hand was on her breast massaging it. Her left hand however was down between her legs, not fingering herself, but actually softly jerking off my cock. She was moaning lightly. "Maybe I should wake him. He might get mad if I were to take my virginity with his cock, but the way he's been rubbing it against me… I'm so wet." She whispered. She positioned the head of my cock at her entrance and let it slip inside her folds. She gasped. "Maybe I should wake him." She said slightly louder. I would've loved for her to take her own virginity with my cock right there and then, and fuck me until I filled her to the brim with cum, not knowing that I was awake. I softly kissed her chocolate shoulder.

"Nah, you don't need to wake me, Caitlin." I whispered. "Now, did you want me to slide it in?" I lifted myself up a bit and looked at her. She was biting her lower lip, a bit indecisive if she wanted me to take it right there on the spot, or make me wait.

"I'll be honest, Josh, I don't know if I'm ready." Caitlin said. She turned her head to look at me. "I mean what if we do it, and then I feel like I've made a mistake… or what if I end up getting pregnant."

"Caitlin, what if you do? Are you ready to join this kind of life? I mean where your lover is shared with his family? Or with other women?" I asked.

"I don't care if you're shared." Caitlin said. "As long as I can have you too." She said.

"Caitlin. I love you. If this is a mistake then it's felt more right than any mistake I've made in the past and it's got even me fooled…" I started, I let out a sigh after saying that and got ready to say the most important part. "And if you get pregnant, wonderful, you'll move in here with us and everyone will help out." I continued. "Or we could get married, and move into our own house were we can raise our children together." I said. Had I really just said that? Was I actually serious? Could this be a mistake? No, it wasn't a mistake. I knew better than that. I wanted nothing more than to be near her. The sex didn't matter to me. We could stop right now and be celibut and I'd be a happy man just content in being around her. But if we did do it, if we made love and I got her pregnant, would I be ready to start a life with her? Well I had enough money built up to move into an apartment and easily pay for everything we needed for the next ten years thanks to the money my father had left me in his will, but marriage? Yeah, that would be awesome, seeing her walking down the aisle in a white dress.

I saw tears welling up in her eyes again. "Oh, Joshua." She said as she slowly slid herself on my cock, pushing past her resistance and taking her own virginity. Her pussy was the tightest yet, and just as hot as Jessi's was the other night. Her walls were clamping down on my cock, to keep it from moving. I was a bit in shock and awe. I leaned in and kissed her as a tear rolled down her cheek. "Make love to me." She whispered. I smiled. I got myself in a proper position to start thrusting in and out of her, but found it difficult, so I pulled out. She immediately caught the cue to switch positions, and into a position on her hands and knees. I got behind her and slid back inside her as much as I could. The truth was, she was tight and wet on her side, but this way was definitely easier on me, but I still couldn't get my entire length inside her with about a couple inches still sticking out. She moaned slightly, but as I slid it out then back in, I found myself fully inside her. "Oh, Joshua! That's so deep!" She moaned. What I didn't know was that I was deeper than I had thought and when thrusting in and out, the head of my penis had pushed against her cervix. She was moaning loudly as I thrust in and out of her. Hitting that same spot over and over.

"Cait... gonna... cum..." I panted. I had been going at a slow pace, but it felt like her walls were milking my cock for every drop they could. "Should... I... pull... out?" I asked.

"No, thrust in hard and cum in that same spot you're hitting!" She yelled.

"Are you sure?" I asked a bit more focused on getting an answer quick.

"Yes. I want it. I want to feel you cuming deep inside me. I love you so much." She moaned. I slammed it in her hard and came, moaning loudly. She moaned too as I felt her body give a slight jerk before she squirted. While we were both moaning from the orgasms we were having, I heard a softer moan from just outside my door. Who was outside my door? Frankly at the moment, I was more concerned with emptying my seed deep in Caitlin's womb. "Yes, Joshua, it feels so right!" She cried out as my cum spurted inside her again and again. Finally after a minute or so of emptying my seed into Caitlin's womb, I pulled out and fell back on my ass. My dick was limp and I was a little light headed. She pulled herself into a sitting position and leaned against me as we heard another soft moan on the other side of the door. She looked at me, then walked over to the door. She opened it, pulling it inwards to find Heather on the other side. She grabbed Heather by the underarm and lifted her up. I turned and looked to see my twin sister standing there, with a t-shirt pulled up around her upper chest revealing her b-cup tits entirely and her underwear around her knees. Caitlin pulled Heather inside and closed the door and locked it. Caitlin was keeping a calm face as she turned back to my twin sister, who just stood there, looking at the ground not trying to cover up in any fashion. Her nipples were small and dark pink and she had a line of pubic hair above her pussy. I wasn't sure if she was waiting for a reaction or what. The inside of her legs were obviously wet from her own juices, as I quickly put two and two together and figured out she had been masturbating listening to us go at it. Caitlin walked around Heather and sat on the bed.

"Well?" Heather asked, expecting to be cussed out.

"Well what?" Caitlin asked. Honestly, I couldn't take my eyes off Heather's body, seeing her naked like that was odd, but felt right. She seemed almost ashamed at being caught doing it.

"Well aren't you gonna cuss me out?" Heather said, lifting her head to look at us. She still made no attempt to cover herself up and just stood there with her arms down at her sides. Caitlin stared at her for a moment then threw her head back laughing. I admit I had to laugh too. Heather looked confused.

"Why would I cuss you out?" Caitlin asked. She turned her head to me. "Do you see any reason to cuss her out?"

"Nope. Why would I?" I said. "It's not like we haven't had sex, or we haven't seen each other naked."

"So you're not mad?" Heather asked in a reluctant tone.

"Why would I be? Heather. We've shared everything. I know, remember?" Caitlin said. Heather had a look of relief on her face.

"I thought you be mad that I was interupting. I mean it is your first time together." Heather said looking down again.

"Know what?" I asked. Caitlin walked over to Heather and gave her a kiss on the lips as she grabbed the bottom of Heather's shirt and lifted it over her head. She then helped Heather remove her panties. She turned to me, blocking my sister from my sight slightly.

"Don't worry. I kinda always felt that I wanted you in on this too." Caitlin said softly. Heather just nodded. Caitlin turned towards Heather and grabbed her by the right hand. She led my sister over to the bed where they both got on it in front of me. Sitting on their knees they began making out like they had been doing it for ages. Holy shit. I was flabbergasted. They broke the kiss.

"Get on your stomach with your hips in the air. I have wanted to try something with you for a long time." Caitlin told Heather. Heather did as she was told, laying down with her chest in Caitlin's pool of fluids on my comforter, right in front of me. Her head was inches from me as she looked back. Caitlin got behind her and began licking and sucking at Heather's pussy. Heather moaned loudly as Caitlin began assaulting her clit, then turned her head towards me. She took my partially hardened member and plunged it in her mouth. I couldn't believe it. My sister was now bobbing her head on my cock. "You love that cock, don't you?" Caitlin teased between licks.

"Yes." Heather said, gasping for air, in between bobs. My eyebrows raised in disbelief. My sister was starting to talk nasty with Caitlin.

"Tell your brother how much you want his cock." Caitlin said. "Tell him what you told me." She pulled my cock from her mouth and began jerking it off, trying to get it fully erect.

"I've wanted you inside me ever since we were teens. That day when Caitlin's top kept coming down, I brushed up against it, and felt you were fully erect. I wanted to have you take my virginity right there. I wanted to feel you fuck me in every way possible. I wanted to see it, feel it, taste it and then I wanted to have you fuck me raw until I couldn't move. I wanted it soft and gentle but rough and hard. I knew you could never take me as your girlfriend, but I always secretly wished you'd make me yours. I stayed celibate waiting to find another guy like you, but there never was one." Heather blurted out before squealing as Caitlin made her cum.

"You're serious?" I asked.

"Yes, Joshy." Heather said, calling me the one and only name she called me when she wanted something. "Caitlin and I used to practice kissing, and I'd get caught up pretending it was you. I'd confess that I wanted you, and she'd help me get off." Heather confessed. Here I was just stunned that my sister was making this kind of confession. "Joshy, please, don't make me wait any longer." She begged.

"You're gonna wait, if you want that cock." Caitlin said. "You're gonna tell him everything."

"No! Caitlin! I can't!" Heather said, her face turning beat red. I couldn't believe it. I had let Caitlin take the driver's seat on this but I mean she is my sister. I could've stopped this at a moment's notice. Told her I wasn't going any further, but I was intrigued. It felt wonderful having her hand on my cock as she told me these things.

"Tell him, or leave. Your choice." Caitlin demanded. She lowered her face back to Heather's nethers and I could only imagine what she was doing back there. Heather squealed again.

"Josh, I've been manipulating your choices here. I don't want you to just take Jessi or Caitlin and have them as your girlfriend. I want to be your girlfriend, your wife, the mother of your children." She confessed. She pulled herself away from Caitlin and positioned herself over me, ready to take my manhood inside her again. "When we did it on the couch, I knew I wasn't ovulating. I always get super horney when I'm ovulating. Joshua. I'm ovulating now. So you can make the decision right now, right here. You can fuck me, and knock me up. There's no chance that you won't today. I've already got myself ready with some drugs from a fertility doctor and everything. Or you can tell me to leave and I'll go find someone else to do it." She said. "I don't care if you still want to fuck the others after this, that's your choice, but I want you to love me as I am, if we're going to do this." She said.

Talk about dropping a bomb on someone. I didn't know what to say. But I knew how I wanted to react. I grabbed her by the hips, and thrust upwards, impaling her completely on my cock. She screamed out in pleasure then laid down on top of me and kissed me on the lips. She pressed her body to mine, she put her arms around my neck and before I realized it her tongue was exploring my mouth. I've heard that it's wrong to love a sibling like this. But when I found my hands exploring my twin sister's body, it felt right as did the kissing. Finally we broke the kiss.

"That took long enough." Caitlin said as Heather put her head against mine as I moved my hands back down to her hips. Heather turned and looked at her.

"You're okay with all of this?" Heather asked.

"Heather. This has got to be…" She started. "The hottest thing I've ever seen." She said.

I looked down. I was buried to the hilt inside her, and could feel myself pressing against her cervix. She could feel it too, or at least I assumed. "I can feel him pressing up against my womb." Heather said to confirm my suspicion. "It feels so perfect." She said.

"I felt that too when he was inside me." Caitlin said. "When he came I could actually feel it filling me up."

"Make love to me." Heather said. My cock was begging me to thrust it in her nice and hard. I wanted to fuck her in every way possible and fill every hole she had with my incestuous seed, but I took it slow, sliding my cock between her lips to find her hole, pressing against her hymen and slowly pushing through it. She yelped as I pushed all the way into her. Buried to the hilt, not something I could do the first time with Caitlin. Looking back I think its because she was just so aroused. "Oh god, it's so deep. It feels so right having you in me like this." She moaned loudly. Caitlin laid down next to her and the two made out as I began thrusting in and out of my twin sister's hole. I started slow but after a few minutes I began working faster and harder. Her pussy was indescribably hot and constantly clenching down on my cock, making it hard to move in and out of her. Which in turn only made me thrust harder and faster. Funny how that works. Caitlin took Heather's right hand and stuck it against her vagina, having Heather start fingering her. I reached to my Sister's left tit and began massaging it for a moment. "Josh! I'm about to!" She tried to warn me but the orgasm she had while I was fucking her was very different from the one she was having before, and she squirted. She cried out as she did so. It was different when she squirted from when Caitlin did. She didn't just squirt out of her clit, she also squirted out of her vagina which covered my balls and cock with her juices. She started crying after she finished cuming. "Oh god, I think I just peed all over you." She said shocked with what happened.

"You squirted." Caitlin explained. "It's not too common, but I've read that anyone can do it. If properly stimulated that is."

"I've never cum like that before." Heather said. "It's okay?" She asked.

"Heather I'm gonna cum." I warned her. Caitlin moved quickly to get on her knees and clamp off my dick and stop me from cuming inside Heather and making me sit up.

"What are you doing?" Heather asked.

"Wait a moment, you two." Caitlin said. "Heather get up." Caitlin helped us get repositioned so I was on top and Heather was underneath me. I began thrusting in and out of her again. It wasn't long before I got close again. I warned Heather quickly.

"Good, cum in her like this, it helps the chances for pregnancy." Caitlin explained. I felt the tip of my cock at her cervix. She let out a long moan as she came again, and my cock exploded harder than it had even with Jessi. I felt it erupt, forcing its way through the tiny hole in her cervix and filling her.

"Oh god! No! It's too much!" Heather cried out. Caitlin kissed her passionately but Heather pulled away, with tears rolling down her cheeks. "Oh god!" She cried. I thought maybe it was a bit uncomfortable for her to have it like this, but I couldn't exactly stop myself from cumming. She screamed out as I could feel her juices squirting again and quickly I realized it wasn't that it was uncomfortable, just too much stimulation for her as her Juices covered my lower body. My cock twitched a few times, then slowly I stopped cuming. I let out a groan of relief and collapsed on top of my twin sister.

"Wow." Caitlin said, looking at me spent. "You came for over three minutes inside her."

"I never thought I'd squirt just from him cuming inside me." Heather panted. I couldn't say a word. I was dizzy, my legs were tingling, and I couldn't really breathe too well.

"Oh god, that was a good idea, Thanks Caitlin." Heather said as I finally pulled myself off of her and my spent cock from her pussy.

"Well I'm ready to go one more time." Caitlin said with a giggle.

"Unfortunately I'm not. I'm gonna need a bit to recuperate." I said. The two ladies looked at each other and giggled.

"Awe, we wore Joshy out." Caitlin said. "Guess I should've had him fuck me more and made you wait longer." She said sarcastically.

"Hey!" Heather said.

"But, in honesty, I think my pussy needs a break too. I'm sore. How about we sit back and watch a movie or two, then we can have some more fun." Caitlin suggested. To be honest, a movie sounded good after all of that hardcore action.

The three of us got dressed, partially, and made our way to the living room. Caitlin popped on some movie and sat opposite Heather and I, which I could tell was driving her nuts, but I just fell asleep again on the couch. Caitlin woke me a few hours later with a kiss on the lips.

"What's going on?" I asked a bit disorientated.

"I have to head back home and go to work silly. Heather already left for her night shift." Caitlin said. "Oh and your mom came home about an hour ago, she had everything figured out in 5 minutes, and told us that we're all adults. Apparently… well no, she told me to have you go and talk to her about that when you woke up." Caitlin said. I was kind of intrigued on what my mother had to say, but Caitlin gave me a lingering kiss, and then headed out the door. I pulled myself to my feet still groggy from it all, and made my way towards the kitchen. My mother was in the dining room as usual, reading a book.

"Oh I see you're finally up." Mom said as she marked her place in her book and set it on the table. I sat down opposite her. "Well it seems like you've got all your ducks in a pond." Mom said. "How have you been holding up?" She asked.

"I'm exhausted, my balls hurt, and I don't know if I can keep fucking this long or this hard." I said.

"Don't worry, you'll get used to it." Mom said. "You know I would've been lucky if my brother had been as caring as you are with your sisters." Mom said. "But I'm sure they'll understand if you need a break."

"What's going on with Becks? I haven't seen her around today." I asked.

"I'm not sure. She and Rachel left early this morning and they haven't gotten back yet." Mom said. I was actually relieved. Two less women in the house meant two less I'd have to satisfy until they got back. Mom was the only one left and she understood where I was at. "As for Heather, I'm not sure if she told you but she took some special…"

"I know. She's trying to get pregnant." I said.

"And you helped. From what I heard. Heather didn't want to go in tonight, but when she called in, they needed her." Mom explained. Heather had been working this job as a Nurse's assistant for nearly a month. If they said they needed her in, they really did.

I excused myself and headed to my room, dropping onto my bed and passing out as soon as I did. The next morning I went out for my usual jog and when I got back I was greeted at my door by someone I didn't suspect. It was an officer.

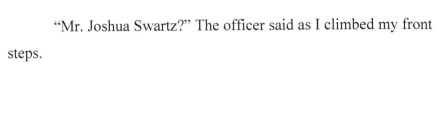

"Mr. Joshua Swartz?" The officer said as I climbed my front steps.

"Yes?" I asked.

"You probably don't remember me. I'm Kyle Truless from your homeroom senior year, I'm doing a friend a favor by coming and finding you personally." The officer said.

"Friend?" I asked.

"Yeah, well, girlfriend. Kira Attah. She's..." Kyle began to say.

"Cait's older sister. Yeah I know. What's going on?" I asked.

"It's bad, Josh. Last night, on her way home from work, Caitlin got in a car accident." Kyle explained.

"What?" I said, my mind reeling. It couldn't be real, it just couldn't.

"Don't worry, she's alive and not too banged up, she'll be home in a few days, but... um... I don't know how to explain this." Kyle said. "She's got amnesia."

"What? What kind?" I asked.

"Not total, she's just lost the last 6 or 7 years of her life. Kira wanted to come here herself, but wanted to stay by Caitlin's side." Kyle explained.

"Oh god. Which hospital?" I asked.

"I'm heading there now, I'll give you a lift in my squad car." Kyle said.

I didn't bother to change, or tell anyone. I left with him, looking back, if it were nowadays, I would've taken my own car, but this was back when you could turn to people and know that you could be more trusting. We got in his car, I actually sat in the front, and he drove me to the hospital. Using his credentials, he got me into the ICU where Caitlin was laying in a bed. She had a black eye and a busted lip, and it took her a moment to recognize me.

"Holy shih. Josh? You got older!" She said, trying to make her words come out correctly.

"Yeah, I hear you got into an accident." I said.

"That's what they tell me, but I don't remember." Caitlin said as I walked over to the side of the bed. "In fact the last thing I remember was getting home from our family day at the beach." She said. "I've tried but it hurts to remember anything else." She said as I took her hand. She looked down and blushed. "Josh, what're you doing?"

"Yesterday, before the accident, you and I finally moved past the friend stage." I said.

"We were boyfriend and girlfriend? Did we kiss?" She asked.

"Yeah, I was your first kiss." I told her, trying not to cry. "You told me that you had been keeping it pent up for so long. Yesterday, we showed each other how much we meant to each other."

"Really? Took us a while, huh?" She asked.

"Yeah. And when you get better and your memories come back, we can pick things up where we left off." I said. Caitlin was officially out of the fun. I wasn't about to fuck a woman who thought she was twelve, no matter how much I cared for her, or wanted her.

"But... but... what if I never get them back?" She asked, almost about to cry.

"Then we'll build new ones together. But right now, I want you to focus on getting better, okay?" I said before giving her a kiss on the cheek. She blushed deeply. "I love you Caitlin. I'll be back to visit you tomorrow, Okay?"

"Okay." She said shyly as the nurse came in and started directing us to leave.

"You all need to leave. Visiting hours are open again tomorrow." The nurse said.

"Joshua?" Caitlin said. I stopped and turned around. "I do love you. I always have. I'm not sure if I told you." She said shyly.

"I love you too, Caitlin. Try to get some rest. We'll talk some more tomorrow." I said. I turned and walked out to the waiting area where her family was now waiting.

"So you and my daughter…" Her mom said.

"Yeah, she and I expressed our feelings yesterday." I said.

"Don't beat around the bush, you two had sex." Tamicka said.

"Yes. We did." I said.

"Well, I'm glad you're not about to take advantage of her like this. She isn't in her normal mind." Kira said.

"I'm not a monster, Kira. Caitlin is special to me. Even if it means I can't be with her in an adult relationship, I'm gonna do what I can to support her getting out of here and back into a normal life again." I said. "Now do we know how her condition is? I mean, if it was just a small accident, the ICU isn't right."

"It wasn't a small accident. She's gonna need surgery to relieve the pressure on her brain." Her mom explained. "Caitlin may not make it through this." I stood there with the realization that she may not be coming out of the hospital. I was heartbroken to think that she might die on me. That I could never love her, date her, or even have children with her. A tear slowly streaked down my face.

"Don't worry, She'll be fine." I said, saying it more for myself than anyone else there. "Cait's a strong woman, and I doubt she'll give up easily."

"Josh is right." Tamicka said. "Let's all make sure we're there for her now." Tamicka came over and gave me a hug as I tried to fight back the tears. "It'll be alright. My big sister will pull through. She'll remember everything too. I just know it. You two will get back together, be happy and have lots of kids."

Chapter 6 – It'll be alright

Tamicka saw to the task of driving me home and wanted all the details of everything that happened between me and Caitlin, but I wasn't in the sharing mood. When we pulled up in front of my house, she grabbed me and pulled me into a passionate kiss. I pushed her off me.

"What the fuck, Tams? I'm with your sister!" I said.

"And yours, and your mom, and Jessi too. And???" She said defiantly. I was caught off guard. Tamicka had been told by someone, I just couldn't guess who. "So what's to stop you from having sex with me?" She asked. Good question.

"I'm not in the mood. Your sister is in the hospital." I said. "And who told you about what we did?"

"Who do you think? Caitlin did. We were planning on surprising you with a threesome this afternoon. But I suppose that can wait." Tamicka said. "I'm sorry about kissing you. I shouldn't have been that forward without telling you what we had planned first."

"It's alright, Tams. I just need some time right now. This is all kind of nuts." I said.

"I understand." She said as I opened the door and stepped out of the car. I walked up to my steps and turned back to watch her drive away. I was kind of blown away by the whole thing. I turned back to my house and walked up the steps and went inside to find Rachel standing there, stretching, in full workout running gear, spandex shorts, a workout top, and her hair in a ponytail, getting ready to head out. She saw the look on my face and knew something was wrong.

"Joshy, what's the matter?" She asked as I dropped onto the couch. She walked over to me. I just sat there, trying to gather my thoughts for a moment as she climbed up on the couch and straddled my lap. She did so in a way that I couldn't look past her. "You need to talk about it, little bro." Rachel said.

"Caitlin got in a bad car accident last night, she may not make it." I said.

"Oh god! What happened? Is she awake? How might she not make it?" Rachel asked.

"According to what I was told by Tams, she hit her head on the steering column. The doctors are going to put her in surgery later today to relieve the pressure on her brain, but it's risky, and on top of that, she has no memory of the past 6 years." I said.

"Oh god, I'm so sorry, Joshy. I knew that she means a lot to you." Rachel said.

"Thanks, Rach, but right now, I just wanna be alone." I said.

"And that's the last thing you need." She said taking me by the hand and standing up. She pulled me to my feet and led me outside and down the street. Soon we were deep in Mr. Stricker's woods.

"Well hey there Champ!" Mr. Stricker said as we walked up to his pool. "I see you brought your sister along." He was in the pool with some woman under water that I couldn't recognize without the pool's underwater lights being on. She was more than likely sucking his cock and would be up in a moment for air.

"Hey, Mr. Stricker." Rachel said.

"What's been going on?" He asked.

"Joshua's having some personal issues, and I was wondering if we could use one of your special zones back here." Rachel asked.

"Sure, though I'd stay away from the sandbox, some wildlife has been using it as a toilet again." He said.

"Will do, and thanks." Rachel said. The woman under the water came back up and needless to say Rachel and I were both surprised when we saw who it was.

"Bert, I'm sorry, but I can't just give you a full blowjob in the pond here." The woman said. Her hair was long and red and she had nothing on. Her tits were a c-36, and I could easily make out her nipples as they poked out of the water.

"Mom?" Rachel said in surprise. The woman turned towards us. It was really her.

"Hi Rachel, Hi Josh." Mom said.

"I'm sure you did have trouble, only a couple have been able to pull off an underwater BJ for me." Mr. Stricker said.

"Mom, what's going on here?" Rachel asked.

"Oh come on Rachel." Mom said rolling her eyes. "You think you were the only one attracted to your brother? Trust me, he's done things that he didn't realize were teasing to me at all from when he turned twelve and started getting older. I had to get release from someone because your brother has his hands full and Bert here has been awesome for it. It's not like I could jump into bed with your brother for all of those years. So I've been seeing Bert for some quickies."

"Mom. You could've come to me at any time." I said.

"Really?" Mom said raising an eyebrow. She swam over to the edge of the pool and pulled herself up showing her muscular body. Her pussy was shaved bald and her tits were impressive in the sunlight.

"Holy shit, mom, you're a babe." Rachel said.

"You think so?" Mom said in disbelief.

"Well, I'm gonna go, I need to get Joshua's mind off things." Rachel said.

"I've worked hard to make this my sanctuary. People can come and go as they please and fuck until they can't fuck anymore." Mr. Stricker said. "Of course some of my things have more therapeutic abilities than others, but why don't you two head to the fort and relax while I have some more fun with your mom."

"Alright, you two have fun now." Rachel said as Mr. Stricker got out of the pool. His cock was large and fully erect. It was a little bigger than mine but he was definitely shaved clean. Rachel grabbed my hand again and led me through the woods until we came upon a small cabin area. She pulled me inside and closed and bolted the door. The interior was made to look like a bunker, with shelves of canned food and water all around us. There was a small bed attached to the wall. "This is the bunker." Rachel said.

I wasn't sure what she had in store for me, but something told me that I was gonna get back in the swing of things.

Epilogue – Wrap up

Thank you for reading the first story in the SWMS series. This has been rewritten to give it more of a story structure than just its original plot of "Everything fucks and sucks!". I certainly hope you enjoyed this version, as there will be added stories to supplement this one. I chose to leave this story on a cliff hanger due to the fact that I want people to enjoy things more. I plan on using what characters appear in the original to help the other novels along.

As it stands now, Joshua has slept with all of his sisters, his mother, Jessi and Caitlin. I know I left out Kira's scenes, but he shouldn't just have a harem at his beck and call. So where does this leave us, well it leaves us with a story with no plot, no development, and frankly, no purpose.

Again, I hope you enjoyed the first story. The next story will appear soon.

Made in the USA
San Bernardino, CA
15 October 2015